Dec...
BARONE...
in Bos...

In addition to our regular flavors of gelato, this month we are featuring:

- **Blueberry tart**

  Gorgeous blue eyes, ebony hair just a tad too long to fit a successful millionaire, broad shoulders and long legs—Steven Conti was drop-dead handsome. But those incredible eyes…the sky-colored orbs went from liquid to flame in an instant, trapping Maria in their heat and stealing her breath….

- **Baby cakes sprinkled with powdered sugar**

  Hiding herself and her unborn child in the snow-dusted pines of Big Sky Country wasn't the answer, but Maria needed time. Time to sort out her feelings and her future. But when Steven found her, she knew the tingling inside her had nothing to do with her pregnancy. She belonged to Steven in a deep, elemental, primitive way….

- **Hot toddies laced with 100 proof rum**

  One kiss from Steven and Maria felt drunk, light-headed, unable to stand. How could she deny herself another night in his arms? But would going to bed with Steven Conti be like sleeping with the enemy? As the Montana winds raged outside, his body heat beckoned. And it was a call she could not deny….

Buon appetito!

Dear Reader,

Thanks for choosing Silhouette Desire, where we bring you the ultimate in powerful, passionate and provocative love stories. Our immensely popular series DYNASTIES: THE BARONES comes to a rollicking conclusion this month with Metsy Hingle's *Passionately Ever After.* But don't worry, another wonderful family saga is on the horizon. Come back next month when Barbara McCauley launches DYNASTIES: THE DANFORTHS. Full of Southern charm—and sultry scandals—this is a series not to be missed!

The wonderful Dixie Browning is back with an immersing tale in *Social Graces.* And Brenda Jackson treats readers to another unforgettable—and unbelievably hot!—hero in *Thorn's Challenge.* Kathie DeNosky continues her trilogy about hard-to-tame men with the fabulous *Lonetree Ranchers: Colt.*

Also this month is another exciting installment in the TEXAS CATTLEMAN'S CLUB: THE STOLEN BABY series. Laura Wright pens a powerful story with *Locked Up With a Lawman*—I think the title says it all. And welcome back author Susan Crosby who kicks off her brand-new series, BEHIND CLOSED DOORS, with the compelling *Christmas Bonus, Strings Attached.*

With wishes for a happy, healthy holiday season,

Melissa Jeglinski

Melissa Jeglinski
Senior Editor, Silhouette Desire

Please address questions and book requests to:
Silhouette Reader Service
U.S.: 3010 Walden Ave., P.O. Box 1325, Buffalo, NY 14269
Canadian: P.O. Box 609, Fort Erie, Ont. L2A 5X3

Passionately Ever After

METSY HINGLE

Silhouette® Desire®

Published by Silhouette Books

America's Publisher of Contemporary Romance

Special thanks and acknowledgment are given to Metsy Hingle for her contribution to the DYNASTIES: THE BARONES series.

For Diane Hingle Anding, sister by marriage & friend by choice

SILHOUETTE BOOKS

ISBN 0-373-76549-5

PASSIONATELY EVER AFTER

Visit Silhouette at www.eHarlequin.com

Printed in U.S.A.

METSY HINGLE

is an award-winning, bestselling author of romance who resides across the lake from her native New Orleans. Married for more than twenty years to her own hero, she is the busy mother of four children. She recently traded in her business suits and a fast-paced life in the hotel and public-relations arena to pursue writing full-time. Metsy has a strong belief in the power of love and romance. She also believes in happy endings, which she continues to demonstrate with each new story she writes. She loves hearing from readers. For a free doorknob hanger or bookmark, write to Metsy at P.O. Box 3224, Covington, LA 70433.

DYNASTIES:
THE
BARONES

Meet the Barones of Boston—
an elite clan caught in a web of danger,
deceit…and desire!

Who's Who in
PASSIONATELY EVER AFTER

Steven Conti—A millionaire by age twenty-five, he had
it all—the prestige, the wealth, the good looks. But he
wanted something he could never have. He wanted…

Maria Barone—The feisty youngest sibling of the
Barone clan, she never ran away from anything in
her life—except Steven. But she had to protect her
heart and her unborn baby from the legendary curse of…

Lucia Conti—Seventy years ago, as a jilted teen,
she called a curse upon the Barones for all eternity.
Was it enduring fact or just a Sicilian superstition?

One

Her luck had just run out.

Steven had found her.

Maria Barone didn't know how she knew that the strange black SUV parked in front of the Calderones' place belonged to Steven. She only knew that she did. Easing her car around the bend in the road, she barely noticed the snow-dusted Ponderosa pines or the darkening December sky. All her thoughts, all her energy, were focused on the impending confrontation. Because she had no doubts whatsoever that there would be a confrontation.

Ever since her cousin Karen had phoned a few days ago to warn her that Steven was searching for her, she'd known it would only be a matter of time before he stumbled onto her hiding place in Silver Valley, Montana. Perhaps that was why from the moment she'd awakened that morning, she'd been plagued by a fluttering in her belly that had nothing to do with the baby growing inside her and everything to do with some sixth sense warning her that her days of eluding Steven Conti were about to come to an end.

Pulling her compact to a stop alongside the empty SUV, Maria sat behind the wheel of her car for several moments. For the space of a heartbeat, she considered turning the vehicle around and leaving to avoid what was bound to be a messy, emotional scene. Just as quickly, she dismissed the idea. She wasn't a coward, she reminded herself firmly. And until recently she'd never run away from a thing in her life. Besides, in another two and a half months Steven and everyone else would know her secret. Determinedly she switched off the car's engine.

All right. Time to face the music.

Mustering her courage, Maria exited the vehicle. After gathering her packages from the back seat, she made her way up the shoveled walkway. When she reached the front door, she drew in a deep breath, filling her lungs with the cool, crisp air in an effort to steady her nerves. She'd known for months now that this day would come—the day when she would have to tell Steven about the baby and lay out her plan for their child's future. Yet she was no closer now to figuring out what that plan entailed than she had been when she'd left Boston more than two months ago. All she knew was that she loved Steven, and she loved her family. And no matter what she decided, someone she loved was going to be hurt. Worse, in choosing, she was going to lose either Steven or her family. Or possibly both.

Maria swallowed hard at that thought. And not for the first time, she wondered why the powers that be had played such a cruel trick on her.

Fate, the voice inside her head whispered. Perhaps it was fate, she thought. How else could she explain that the man she'd fallen in love with was a Conti—the one man in the world with whom she couldn't possibly share a future? Maria sighed at the futility of her situation. No matter how much she might wish for things to be different, the past could not be changed. The Contis and the Barones were sworn enemies, had been enemies long before either she or Steven had been born. And the feud between their families that had begun when Marco Barone had eloped with her grandmother instead of marrying Steven's Aunt Lucia was just as strong now as it had been nearly seventy years ago. In truth, the bad blood was probably even stronger now, Maria conceded, as she recalled all the misfortunes that had befallen the Barone family as a result of the Conti curse.

The Conti curse.

Maria shuddered at the thought of that horrid curse that had plagued her family for nearly seven decades. Even now, she still could recall sitting at her grandmother's knee as a young girl and listening to the story of the Conti curse. She could almost hear her grandmother's voice explaining....

"Lucia was so angry, so bitter, when Marco and I told them we were married," Angelica Barone said as she related the tale of their elopement and how they had gone to the Contis and pleaded with them to understand.

"Understand?" a furious Lucia countered. *"I understand that you have betrayed me, my brother and our family."*

"We love each other," Marco Barone had told her. *"I never meant to hurt you, Lucia."*

"Well, you have hurt me. You have hurt all of the Contis."

"Perhaps someday when you are older, you will understand and be able to forgive us and wish us happiness," Angelica offered.

"I shall never forgive you," Lucia spat out. *"And I shall never wish you any happiness. In fact, I curse you. You got married on Valentine's Day, so from this day forward, I wish you and all of your descendants a lifetime of miserable Valentine's Days—just like the miserable one you gave me."*

Then exactly one year later on the first anniversary of their wedding, Angelica Barone had miscarried the child she had been carrying. Maria shuddered again at the memory of her grandmother and the sadness that crept into her eyes when she had told her about losing her first child.

Smoothing a protective hand over her stomach, Maria couldn't help worrying again how that curse might affect the baby growing inside her—a baby due on Valentine's Day. Despite Steven's claim that the tragedies her family had suffered were coincidences and that the Conti curse was nothing more than superstition fueled by overactive imaginations, Maria knew he was wrong. She had only to look at this past year for proof that the curse was real and the unhappiness that Lucia Conti had called down upon all Barones was continuing to wreak havoc.

Biting her lower lip, Maria considered the disasters that had plagued her family during the past year—disasters that all commenced shortly after she'd become involved with Steven. She winced at the memory of the sabotage of the new passionfruit gelato on Valentine's Day and the turmoil of bad press and lost revenue that had resulted. Then there had been the fire at the plant and her cousin Emily's amnesia. And worst and most frightening of all had been the recent kidnapping of both Steven's sister, Bianca, and her cousin Derrick.

Perhaps Steven could dismiss the curse, but she couldn't, Maria admitted. Besides, even if she were able to get past her fears of the curse, how would she ever be able to get past the loss of her family? How would Steven get past losing his family? Because she had no doubts that both families would disown them were she and Steven to declare that they wanted to share their lives together.

She'd grown up in the bosom of her large, boisterous family and wanted the same for her baby. For her and Steven to be together, she would have to forfeit that joy. How could she possibly condemn her baby to a life in which he or she would be stripped of that love? How could she possibly allow her baby to become caught up in the ongoing feud between the Barones and Contis?

The fact was, she couldn't. She wouldn't. For her baby's sake, she would have to be strong, Maria told herself again. Somehow she had to find a way to reason with Steven, to make him see that they could have no future together because too many people would be hurt. And the one who would suffer the most would be their child. She simply had to make him see that.

Squaring her shoulders, Maria shifted her packages under her arm and reached for the doorknob. As usual, she found the house unlocked. Quickly, before she changed her mind, she hurried inside out of the cold. And for the first time since she'd arrived over two months ago, the scents of the baking bread and burning wood did nothing to soothe her spirit. Nor did the sound of Magdalene's and Louis Calderone's laughter coming from somewhere inside the house.

"Then my Aunt Lucia said…"

Maria started at the deep rumble of Steven's voice and sent one of the wrapped boxes from her shopping bag tumbling to the floor.

"Oh, that must be Maria now," Magdalene said.

Chastising herself for reacting like a clumsy schoolgirl at just the sound of Steven's voice, Maria retrieved the fallen package and began stuffing it into her shopping bag.

"Maria? Is that you?"

"It is either Maria or a clumsy burglar," Louis joked, his Spanish ancestry apparent in his speech.

"Maria?" Magdalene called out again.

"Yes, Magdalene. It's me," Maria replied, surprised that she managed to sound almost normal when nerves were tap-dancing in her stomach. "I'll be there in a minute," she added as she tried to calm herself.

But Magdalene was already rushing out to the foyer to greet her. "You were gone so long. Louis and I were about to send out a search party to look for you."

"I'm sorry if I worried you," Maria told her. "I decided to do some Christmas shopping while I was in town."

"So I see," Magdalene told her as she eyed the bags stuffed with gifts. "And your doctor visit?" she asked as she removed the shopping bag and packages from her fingers and set them aside. "Everything is okay?"

"Yes. Yes, everything is fine," Maria told her as she stripped off her gloves and jammed them inside her coat pocket. She removed the scarf bundled around her neck and before she could protest, Magdalene was reaching for it and draping it over the coatrack beside the door.

"Here, give me your coat," Magdalene instructed.

"No," Maria said sharply, then immediately softened her voice. "I mean I want to keep it on for a while.

I…I'm still feeling a little chilled,'' she fibbed, deciding to delay the inevitable a bit longer by hiding her body beneath the voluminous coat.

Magdalene reached for Maria's fingers and frowned. ''It is no wonder you are cold. Your hands, they are like ice. Are you sure you feel all right, *la pequeña?*''

For once Maria didn't bother pointing out to the tiny, dark-haired woman that since she was a full two inches taller than Magdalene and her stomach was beginning to resemble a basketball, the pet name ''little one'' really didn't suit her. ''I'm fine. Really. The sun's beginning to go down, so it's turned colder outside. That's all,'' she offered in explanation. ''I just need a few minutes to warm up and I'll be fine.''

Apparently satisfied, Magdalene said, ''All right. If you are sure.''

''I'm sure,'' Maria informed her.

''Then, come. I have a surprise for you. A visitor,'' she added, her eyes sparkling. She turned and started toward the den.

But Maria remained frozen to the spot.

''Maria?'' Magdalene said when she realized that she wasn't following. ''You are sure you are okay?''

''Yes, I'm fine.''

''Then come, *pequeña,*'' Magdalene urged and motioned for her to follow. She ushered her toward the den. In a voice filled with glee she announced, ''Look who has come all the way from Boston just to see you.''

Even though Maria had known before setting one foot into the room that she would find Steven waiting there, that knowledge didn't lessen the impact of seeing him again. Just as it had that very first time when their eyes had met across the room at Nicholas and Gail's wedding reception nearly a year ago, the air seemed to back up in Maria's lungs. She hadn't known back then that Steven was a Conti. All she had known was that never before in her life had she been so drawn to a man. More than drawn, she admitted. She'd been entranced by him. One look and she'd known that he was the man she had waited for her entire life. She drank in the sight of him again now. The tall, athletic frame of his body. Those linebacker shoulders that filled the black and red sweater he wore so wonderfully. The tad-too-long dark hair that made him look more like a rebel than a dot-com millionaire. Suddenly Maria could remember all too easily the texture of his hair when she'd wound her fingers through it, the feel of that hair brushing against her bare skin while they made love.

Realizing what she was doing, Maria shut off the dangerous memories. She lifted her gaze to meet Steven's. And her breath hitched as those piercing blue eyes of his went from cool to hot as he looked at her. For a moment, Maria couldn't breathe. Trapped in the heat of his gaze, her pulse pounded frantically as Steven started across the room toward her. His eyes never wavered and when he captured her nervous fingers in his hands, Maria feared for a moment that she might actually faint.

"Hello, Maria," he said, his voice like a caress.

Maria opened her mouth, intent on returning the greeting, but no words came out. As though in a trance, she simply stood there and watched as Steven began to lower his head. When his mouth was mere inches from hers, sanity suddenly came slamming back. She turned her face away and his lips brushed her cheek. The kiss was light, barely a whisper of a touch, but it might as well have been a brand, Maria thought, because she felt the burn of Steven's kiss all the way down to her toes.

Rattled and fearful she would do something foolish

like throw herself into his arms, Maria pulled her hands free and stepped back. "Hello, Steven," she finally managed and didn't miss the flicker of annoyance that crossed his handsome face.

"It is a lovely surprise, your Steven coming to visit you, yes?" Magdalene asked

"Somehow I don't think Maria's all that surprised to see me, Mrs. Calderone," Steven offered in her silence.

"It is Magdalene," her friend chided him.

"My apologies, Magdalene," Steven offered gallantly and earned another smile from the older woman.

"This is true, Maria? You were expecting Steven?" Magdalene asked.

"No, not exactly," Maria hedged. More like she had hoped that he wouldn't be able to find her. Aware that both Magdalene and Louis were waiting for her to explain, she said, "When I spoke to Karen the other day she mentioned that Steven had said he wanted to speak with me."

Steven arched his brow at her understatement. But much to her relief he didn't point out that he had sworn to Karen that he intended to track her down no matter how long it took him.

Unfortunately, it hadn't taken him long at all. Not that she was surprised, she wasn't. After all, Steven Conti hadn't become a millionaire before he was twenty-five by failing to attain whatever goal he'd set for himself. And according to Karen, he had been quite determined to find her—with or without her cousin's help.

"Well, Louis and I are happy you have come. Our Maria has been moping about since Thanksgiving. Now we understand why. Don't we, Louis?" Magdalene asked, the twinkle back in her eyes.

"We do?" Louis asked, a puzzled expression on his dark, weathered face.

Magdalene rolled her eyes. "Men! Louis, our Maria has not only been missing her family. She has been missing Steven."

"Is Magdalene right, Maria? Have you missed me?" Steven asked, his voice somber, his eyes serious.

Her heart ached at the longing he made no attempt to hide from her. Not trusting herself to answer him, she turned away and walked over to the fireplace. For once she failed to appreciate the beauty of the Indian blanket that hung on the wall above the stone hearth. She simply stared into the fire, scarcely aware of the heat of the flames that licked at the logs or the spit and hiss of the burning wood. She pressed a hand to her belly and searched for the right words to tell Steven about the baby.

"*Pequeña,* what is wrong?" Magdalene asked. "Maria?"

At the sound of Magdalene's voice, Maria shook off her sadness and turned her attention toward the other woman. "I'm sorry, Magdalene. Did you say something?"

A frowning Magdalene marched over to her, placed a hand on her forehead, then caught her fingers. "No fever. And you don't feel chilled anymore. Are you still cold?"

"A little," Maria fibbed, still unwilling to reveal her protruding belly.

Magdalene's frown deepened. "Did you tell the doctor about these chills?"

"Doctor?" Steven repeated and Maria didn't miss the note of alarm in his voice. "What's this about a doctor? Are you sick?"

"No. No, I'm not sick. It was just a checkup," Maria said quickly, silently pleading with Magdalene with a look to say nothing about the baby. "I'm just not used to the Montana winters and I was a little chilled when I came inside. That's all."

Magdalene's dark eyes widened slightly as understanding dawned. "Perhaps some hot chocolate will help to warm you up," she offered, but Maria didn't miss the reproach in the other woman's expression.

"Yes. Hot chocolate sounds wonderful," Maria replied.

"What about you, Steven?" Magdalene asked as she returned to the coffee table and began loading dishes onto the serving tray. "Would you care for another cup of coffee or would you like hot chocolate, too?"

"If it's no trouble, coffee would be great."

"No trouble at all."

"I'll take another cup, too," Louis informed his wife.

"Why don't you come help me in the kitchen, Louis?" Magdalene suggested.

"But—"

"I'm sure Steven and Maria have much to discuss. You will excuse us for a moment. Yes?" Magdalene asked and gave Maria a pointed look.

"Of course," Maria said.

"Come, Louis." Magdalene smiled at her confused-looking spouse and handed him the tray. "Perhaps you will sample the cinnamon rolls I baked earlier. I am thinking that maybe I should send some for the Christmas Bazaar at the church."

"Anything to help you and the church," a beaming Louis replied, and with tray in hand, he headed for the door.

Magdalene paused, looked back at Maria for a moment. "I will be in the kitchen if you need me, *pequeña*," she said before following her husband from the room.

Steven watched the two women exchange looks and wondered at the unspoken message that passed between them. For a moment, he could have sworn he'd picked up some strange vibes in the room, but then Magdalene was closing the door and leaving him alone with Maria.

With the Calderones gone, the room fell silent, and were it not for the hiss of the logs burning in the fireplace, Steven was sure he could have heard a pin drop. But after months of being haunted by the memory of Maria, not even the unnatural silence dimmed the pleasure of being near her again.

So he drank in the sight of her now. Like a starving man, he took in every detail of her appearance. Her hair was longer, he noted, falling like mahogany silk nearly to her shoulders. Her skin was paler than he remembered, but there seemed to be a glow to it now that hadn't been there when she'd fled from Boston. Courtesy of the mountain air, he suspected. He wasn't sure if the flush in her cheeks was due to his presence or to the heat from the fire, and decided it was probably a little of both.

He looked into those big doe eyes of hers—eyes that he'd seen countless times in his dreams. Much to his disappointment there was the same wariness in them now that had been there the last time he'd seen her. Shrugging off his disappointment, Steven stared at her mouth. Her mouth was the same—still sultry and tempting. He couldn't help remembering how perfectly that mouth had fit with his. How it had felt to hear those lips crying out his name when he was buried deep inside her.

How those same lips had sworn that she loved him. He wanted to go to her, pull her into his arms and kiss her, hear her say those words to him again now. And because he wanted to so badly, he jammed his fists into his pockets to keep from reaching for her.

"How did you find me?" she asked, breaking the silence.

"Does it really matter? The important thing is that I did find you," he told her, not wanting to admit that he'd broken a few rules in his quest to locate her. When she said nothing, he released a breath in exasperation. "I tracked you through your credit card. You used it to send flowers to your family for Thanksgiving."

"But how—" she began, only to answer the question herself. "The computer. You hacked into the computer system for my credit card activity."

"Yes," he admitted. "And if you're going to tell me that what I did was illegal, don't bother. I already know that. But I was desperate to find you."

"You could have been arrested."

Steven shrugged. "It would have been a small price to pay."

"You shouldn't have risked it," she charged.

"I would have risked a lot more than that to find you," he said honestly. "But it seems I got away with my crime. That is, unless you're planning to turn me in."

"Of course I'm not," she countered.

"For a minute there, I wasn't sure," he teased, wanting to lighten the mood. Much to his regret, Maria continued to look grim. "Now that I've answered your question, how about answering mine?"

Maria wrinkled her brow, causing the tiny crease

along her forehead he'd noted whenever she was puzzling over something. "What question?"

"Was Magdalene right? Did you miss me?" When she said nothing, Steven bit back the sting of disappointment and his voice was hard as he said, "It's a simple question, Maria. All it requires is a yes or no answer. Did you miss me? Even just a little bit?"

"Yes. I've missed you," she said finally, the words little more than a whisper.

Relief rushed through him at her reply and he started toward her. "God, Maria, if you only knew how much—"

"Don't," she said, holding up her hand.

Steven stopped in his tracks. Frustration churned inside him. Frustration and hurt. "Don't what, Maria? Don't tell you that I love you? That I've been going out of my mind these past two months without you? That I believed you when you said that you loved me? And that you damn near cut my heart out when you ran off like you did without any explanation?"

"I left you a note," she defended.

"Yeah, a few paltry lines saying that you needed to get away. That you needed time to think," he said, not bothering to keep the bitterness from his voice. He paced the length of the room, jammed a fist through his hair. He whipped back around to face her. "How do you think that made me feel? I tell you that I love you, that I want to marry you and then you disappear and tell me not to try to find you. Do you have any idea how much that hurt me?"

"I'm sorry."

"You're sorry?" he repeated and marched over to where she stood before the fireplace hearth. "You say you love me, then rip my heart out and throw it back in my face by running away, and all you have to say is that you're sorry?''

She stared up at him out of sad brown eyes. ''Believe me, Steven. Hurting you was…is the last thing I ever wanted to do.''

''Well, you did hurt me,'' he fired back. Unable to stop himself, he reached for her. ''I love you, Maria. And dammit, I know you love me. So why are you doing this to us? Tell me what's wrong. Whatever it is, I'll fix it.''

''You can't fix it,'' she said and pulled away from him. Hugging her arms to herself, she turned her back to him and stared into the fire. ''No one can fix it. No one.''

The tears in her voice ripped at him. ''What is it, love? Tell me what's wrong.''

When Maria shook her head, he turned her around to face him. Tipping up her chin, he stared into eyes bright with tears and secrets. A fist seemed to tighten itself around his heart as he studied her face. He'd always thought Maria beautiful—from the first moment he'd set eyes on her at Nicholas and Gail's wedding. Yet there was something even more beautiful about her now, an inner glow much like the waitress at his family's restaurant when she'd been—

Steven yanked his gaze from Maria's and moved down the length of her body. Emotion churned inside him as he registered the subtle differences in her appearance and demeanor. He took in the shapeless red coat that swallowed her slender frame, noted the protective way Maria's hands rested near her middle. In the blink of an eye, all the changes in her hit him like a sucker punch. ''Take off your coat, Maria,'' he commanded in a voice so controlled and cool, it sounded foreign even to him.

She stared at him, like a deer that had been caught in the headlights of an oncoming car, he thought. And he hated the fact that it was fear that he read in her eyes. ''Steven—''

''Take off the coat, Maria,'' he repeated and softening his voice, he added, ''Please.''

With a patience that belied the blood racing like wildfire through his veins, Steven watched as she slowly unbuttoned the red coat. When the last button had been loosened, she pulled off the coat and tossed it aside. She lifted her head, angled her gaze up to his and stared at him out of eyes bright with defiance.

Steven lowered his gaze and stared at her protruding stomach. Emotions pummeled through him at breakneck speed—anger, joy, hurt. When he lifted his gaze to meet hers again, he read the regret in her eyes. And it was that regret that sent a knife plunging straight through his heart.

''Tell me something, Maria,'' he said, taking care to keep his voice soft while rage and pain warred inside him.

''What?''

''Were you even planning to tell me that I was going to be a father?''

Two

For a moment, Maria couldn't speak. In the time she'd known Steven, she'd discovered a man with many layers. The smart, ambitious businessman who'd made his first million before he'd turned twenty-five. The kind and caring man who loved his family as fiercely as she loved her own. The passionate and tender lover to whom she'd given her virginity and her heart. But never once, not even when she'd refused to take their relationship public or to discuss his offer of marriage, had she seen Steven like this—in a white-hot fury made all the more chilling because he kept it so tightly leashed.

Anger emanated from every pore of his being. It was there in the tight lines around his mouth, in the ticking of the muscle in his right cheek, in the hard set of his jaw. Despite her sweater and the heat of the fire, Maria shivered beneath his icy blue glare. Not because she feared Steven would harm her physically. She didn't.

She knew he would sooner cut off his arm than hurt any woman. But the contempt she read in his eyes struck her like a blow.

"It's a simple question, Maria. I'd appreciate an answer."

Maria's head swam. Squeezing her eyes shut, she wrapped her arms around herself and fought to steady herself, searched for the right words to explain.

"Look at me, Maria," he commanded in a voice so soft she had to strain to hear it. "Were you even planning to tell me about the baby? Or did you think I didn't deserve to know I was going to be a father?"

She snapped her eyes open and forced herself to meet his gaze. "Of course you deserved to know," she told him. "And I was going to tell you."

"When?" he demanded. "After the baby was born? What were you going to do? Send me a birth announcement and tack on a note saying 'By the way, congratulations, you're a daddy'?"

Maria wanted to cringe beneath the contempt in his voice, but she forced herself to face his anger. After all, she reasoned, he was entitled to be furious with her. She'd had months to get used to the idea of becoming a parent while Steven…Steven had been blindsided by the news because she'd kept silent. "No. I was going to tell you before the baby was born. I swear I was," she said, hoping he believed her. "I never intended to keep it from you, Steven. I've been wanting to tell you for months now—almost from the moment I found out that I was pregnant."

"Then why didn't you?" he asked, anguish in his voice, in his eyes. "Dammit, Maria! How could you lay in my arms, make love with me and tell me that you love me, and then keep something like this a secret?"

Maria ached for him. She ached for herself and for all the pain they had both suffered during the past few months. Lifting her hand, she touched his cheek. "I didn't want to keep it a secret. I wanted to tell you. I just didn't know how."

Some of the fierceness in his expression eased at her words. He turned his mouth into her palm and kissed it. At the gentle touch of his lips, Maria's heart swelled with love for him. Oh, how she loved him, she thought. She stared at his handsome face—the sharp angles of his jaw, the proud chin, the sweep of dark lashes that covered his too-serious blue eyes. In the firelight, his black hair gleamed like polished onyx and she had to quell the urge to brush back that errant strand that always fell across his forehead. Instead she somehow found her voice and said, "I'm sorry. I never meant for you to find out about the baby this way. I had hoped...I had planned—"

"Shh. It doesn't matter now," he said and reached for her other hand. His eyes never left hers as he brought her fingers to his lips and kissed them again. "All that matters is that we're together now, and that we're going to have a baby. A baby," he repeated, his voice filled with awe. "I still can't believe it. We're actually going to have a baby."

"Steven—"

He silenced her with a kiss. "Do you have any idea what I've been going through these past months? All the things that went through my head when you left that note and disappeared. I was so angry with your family. I was sure that they had found out about us and forced you to go away."

"No, they didn't," she began. "It wasn't them. It was me. It was all my idea."

"Yeah. I figured that out after talking to Karen last week. But there was a part of me that didn't want to believe you could do that—just up and leave me the way you did, not after what we'd shared."

Guilt tugged at her. "It wasn't easy. I…I didn't know what else to do. I thought if I could get away, that if I had some time alone to think…"

"That's what Karen said. But it didn't stop me from worrying that maybe you'd had second thoughts about us, that you'd begun to believe the things your family had been saying about the Contis sabotaging Baronessa Gelati. I thought…I was afraid that you hated me. That you'd regretted what we'd shared." He swallowed and continued, "I was afraid that you'd regretted loving me."

"No," she told him honestly, and unable to stop herself, she brought her palm to his cheek. When he once again turned his face and kissed her palm, she didn't withdraw. Regret loving him? No, she thought. It would have been easier for her to not take her next breath than to ever regret falling in love with him. Growing up with both her grandparents and parents as examples of what real love was all about, she knew what she felt for Steven was real. In fact, she doubted that she'd even had a choice when it came to loving him. She simply did— had almost from the moment they'd first met. And while she regretted the problems and the heartache their love would cause their families, she couldn't ever regret the love they'd found with each other. How could she when the child growing inside was a result of that love? Their baby was a beautiful miracle, a gift she would always cherish, just as she would always cherish having been loved by Steven. "I've never regretted loving you. Never. Not even for a minute."

"Thank God," he said, and as though her reply had opened some floodgate of emotion inside him, he pulled her into his arms.

After so many months without him, Maria reveled in the feel of Steven's arms around her again. This time when he lowered his head to kiss her, she made no attempt to deny him or herself.

His mouth closed over her own. Steven kissed her—tenderly, passionately, hungrily. When his tongue tested the seam of her lips, Maria didn't hesitate. She opened to him. Tongues explored, danced, mated. He kissed her and kissed her, each thrust of his tongue fueling the need for more. By the time he tore his mouth free and groaned, Maria felt dazed. Awash in emotion and sensations, she clutched at his shoulders, fearful her knees would buckle at any moment. Then his clever, oh-so-clever mouth began to kiss the shell of her ear. Tiny, nibbling kisses that made her heart race and her blood heat. When he nipped the lobe of her ear, Maria sucked in a breath.

It was a mistake, she realized as she breathed in his familiar scent. Suddenly her senses were flooded with the smell of him. He smelled of soap and fresh snow and the forest. And Maria couldn't help but think of how many times during the past few months those scents had triggered memories of him, had made her ache to be in his arms again like this.

When Steven began planting a string of kisses along her jawline, Maria knew she was playing a dangerous game. She wanted Steven desperately, loved him just as fiercely. Yet there could be no future for them. She knew it, had known it almost from the start. Not even the baby growing inside her could change the impossibility of them sharing a life together. To allow Steven to continue would only make him believe otherwise. And to do so would be wrong, she reasoned. "Steven," she began, knowing she had to tell him to stop.

But then he kissed her neck and the protest died on her lips. Tipping her head back, she gave him the access he sought. As he kissed her throat, the hint of whiskers along his jaw felt like fine sandpaper brushing against her softer skin. The sensation was erotic, seductive. When Steven flicked his tongue across her sensitized flesh, Maria nearly whimpered. She curled her fingers into his sweater, marveled at the feel of hard muscle and sinew beneath the soft cashmere.

"So sweet, so incredibly sweet," he murmured, his breath a warm rush against her fevered skin. Her heart pounded so wildly in her chest, Maria feared it would burst at any second.

When Steven nudged aside the V-neckline of her sweater and shirt to kiss her collarbone, her breath hitched. Sliding her fingers through his hair, she pulled his head up and brought his mouth back to her own.

This time when their lips met, it was Maria who groaned as he nipped at her lower lip and took control of the kiss. Maria's head swam beneath the onslaught of his mouth and tongue, the feel of his hands sliding down her back, over her hips. When he cupped her bottom and lifted her, pressed her against his arousal, Maria trembled.

"God, Maria, I've missed you so much," he said as he continued to pepper her face with kisses.

"And I've missed you," she admitted, lost in the feel of his mouth and hands on her after so long without him. "I'm sorry I didn't tell you about the baby...that I ran away like I did...."

"I told you, it doesn't matter," he said, cutting off her apology with another earth-shattering kiss.

When he lifted his head, Maria could have sworn the world had tilted beneath her feet. In an effort to steady herself, she looped her arms around his neck and only then did she realize that Steven was carrying her toward the couch.

Gently he placed her atop the cushions and sat beside her. She'd barely had time to register what had happened when he cupped her face in his hands. He pressed a kiss to her forehead and said, "The only thing that matters is that we're together now. I swear, I won't let anything ever keep us apart again."

His words were like a dash of cold water, instantly sobering Maria. "Steven," she began.

"I swear to you, Maria, I'm going to be the very best husband and father," he continued.

"Steven, don't," she said and struggled to sit up.

"What is it? Is it the baby? Did I hurt you or the baby?"

"No. No, the baby's fine. I'm fine," she assured him.

"Then what is it? What's wrong?"

"We need to slow down. Everything is happening too fast," Maria told him.

Steven's gaze slid from her face to her belly. "Sweetheart, from where I'm sitting, I think we need to move fast," he said, a note of humor in his voice. "When's the baby due?"

"In February," Maria said. "On Valentine's Day, February fourteenth." She waited several heartbeats for him to acknowledge the ominous date.

He didn't. Instead, he said, "Then we don't have much time to plan the wedding. I'll be honest, I'd just as soon we elope right now with just Magdalene and Louis as our witnesses.''

''Steven, please.''

''But if you've got your heart set on a big wedding, I understand,'' he said, ignoring her protest. ''I have only one condition, that we get married before Christmas. I want us to start the New Year as husband and wife.''

''Stop it!''

He jerked back as though she'd slapped him, and narrowed his eyes. ''Stop what, Maria?''

''Stop trying to railroad me into marrying you.''

Steven stood, but continued to stare down at her with accusing eyes. ''Is that what I'm doing? Railroading you into a marriage you don't want?'' He didn't give her a chance to answer. Instead, he continued, ''I love you, and I thought you loved me.''

''I do love you,'' she told him, feeling frustrated and confused. It was the truth. She did love Steven with all of her heart.

He knelt down beside her and captured her hands in his. ''Then marry me, make a life with me and our baby.''

She tugged her hands free and looked away. ''You know it's not that simple.''

''I know it's not that difficult either. Most people who love each other and are expecting a baby get married.''

''We're not most people,'' she reminded him. ''I'm a Barone and you're a Conti.''

''And our baby will be both,'' Steven pointed out as he stood once more.

''I know that. It's just—''

''We can make this work, Maria,'' he insisted. ''I

know we can. We'll get married and you can move into
my apartment. Or we can buy a house and—''

''Don't,'' Maria cried out, unable to bear having
Steven describe a life for the two of them that she knew
in her heart wasn't possible. Tears stung her eyes. And
she immediately blamed those threatening tears on her
body's hormones—hormones that had been out of whack
since she'd become pregnant. Because she was afraid if
she admitted the truth—that she wanted the life with him
that Steven had described—she would weaken. And she
couldn't afford to weaken now. Not when there was so
much at stake. Deciding she needed distance in order to
clear her senses and think rationally, Maria said, ''I think
it would be best if you were to leave now.''

''Forget it. I'm not going anywhere.''

''Then you'll have to excuse me,'' she said primly.

But Steven didn't move a muscle. He simply stood
there, looking tall and daunting as he stared down at her.

''Please get out of my way,'' she said firmly, coolly.

His expression hardened and for a moment she
thought he would refuse. Then he stepped aside and offered her his hand. Maria hesitated, then admitting that
her added bulk from the baby made getting up more
difficult, she accepted his help. But once on her feet, she
quickly pulled away and hurried past Steven. She walked
over to the fireplace. As she stared into the flames, she
searched for the right words to make him understand that
she couldn't marry him. A marriage between the two of
them would never work. How could it when their union
would rip apart both of their families? Worse, she feared
they would only end up hating each other.

''If you think giving me that ice-princess routine is
going to make me give up, then you don't know me as

well as I thought you did. I'm not leaving here until I get the answer I want, Maria.''

And she wanted to give him the answer he wanted. Because it was what she wanted, too. Only she couldn't do that. Not with the threat of the curse hanging over her and their unborn child. The idea of something happening to her own baby sent a surge of panic through her, and before she could stop herself, a sob escaped her lips.

''Damn,'' Steven muttered. He could just kick himself for causing Maria to cry. And although he couldn't see her face, he'd bet his last dollar that Maria was already regretting that outburst of tears. He knew her well enough to know that she would consider those tears a show of weakness. But then, Maria had always been her own harshest critic, he thought. Probably the result of having a family that expected far too much of her.

It simply wasn't fair. Why did she have to be the one designated to carry on Angelica Barone's legacy? Why couldn't someone else run the popular Baronessa Gelateria in Boston's North End? Why did it have to be Maria? There certainly were enough Barones to share the load. But no, for some reason, they all dumped it on Maria's shoulders. And as far as he was concerned, the entire lot of them had taken advantage of her for far too long. It simply had to stop.

He stared at Maria's slender shoulders, could only imagine the enormous weight of responsibility they carried. Not only had she been burdened with the problems of running the gelateria and trying to live up to everyone's expectations of her, but she'd also had to face the pregnancy alone. He should have realized what was wrong long before now, he told himself as his own guilt escalated. But instead of helping her and relieving some of that stress she was under, he'd only managed to add to it. The realization made him feel ten times worse.

Regretful for having upset her, Steven moved behind Maria and placed his hands on her shoulders. "I'm sorry," he said softly. "You know I'd sooner cut off my arm than hurt you. I hate knowing that I've made you cry."

"You didn't. Make me cry, I mean. I'm not crying," she fibbed even as she swiped at her eyes.

"Well, that's a relief." Hoping to lighten the mood, he quipped, "Because when a fellow tells a girl he loves her and asks her to marry him, tears aren't exactly the reaction he's hoping for."

"Oh, Steven, I'm sorry," she said, tears once again in her voice.

Steven sighed. Since his attempt at levity hadn't worked, he tried honesty instead. "Is the idea of marrying me so awful?"

"No," she said and he didn't miss the hand swiping at her eyes again.

"Then why the tears?"

"I've got something in my eye. Probably just an eyelash," she offered in explanation.

"Want me to take a look?" he asked, hoping to get her to turn around and look at him.

"Thanks, but it's out now. I...I'm all right."

"You don't sound all right. You sound sad, and I don't ever remember you being sad—not even when things were a mess." Even amidst the disaster of the new flavor launch in February when she'd had plenty of reason to cry, she hadn't shed a single tear. Nor had she given any indication of feeling defeated—not like she was doing now.

She let out an audible breath. "It's my hormones. The pregnancy has them all messed up."

"I think we both know it's more than just hormones at work here." When she didn't respond, Steven squeezed her shoulders. "Talk to me, Maria. Whatever it is, I promise we'll work it out."

"We can't work it out."

"How do you know if you won't at least talk to me?" he asked. When she still remained silent, he pleaded, "I love you. Please, don't shut me out."

"I'm not shutting you out."

"Aren't you? What do you call running away from Boston the way you did?"

"I didn't run away." She straightened her spine and stepped away from his touch. Picking up the fire poker, she prodded at the logs in the grate. "I told you, I needed to get away. I wanted some time to think, to figure out what I should do about the baby."

Steven froze at her remark. Stunned he took a moment to find his voice. "You can't mean that you considered…that you even thought for a minute about getting rid of…"

"No!" She whipped her gaze from the fire over to him. "How could you even think such a thing?"

"You're right. I'm sorry. It's just that for a minute I thought…" Steven rubbed the back of his neck. "I don't know what I thought. I obviously wasn't thinking straight."

"You obviously weren't thinking at all. If you had, you'd know that I would never do anything to harm my baby."

"*Our* baby," he corrected.

She didn't comment, simply turned her attention back to the fire. "Anyway, I left Boston because I needed some time by myself so I could figure out how I'm going to handle things.''

''You mean how *we're* going to handle things, don't you?'' Steven asked because he fully intended to be a part of her and their baby's future.

When his question was met with silence, Steven took the poker from Maria's fingers and set it aside. Then he turned her around so that she was forced to look at him. But one look at her face and he realized she was under even more strain than he'd first thought. Tear streaks stained her pale cheeks and there was a sadness in those big brown eyes that ripped at him. He wanted to take her in his arms, kiss her and tell her not to worry. That he would handle everything. That he would take care of her and their baby.

Yeah right, Conti.

Considering that mile-wide independent streak of hers, he'd be damned lucky to even get the words out before she tore a strip off of him. And then she'd be even more determined to deal with everything on her own. Well, Maria wasn't the only one with a stubborn streak. He had one, too. And he had no intention of letting her call all the shots. Besides, he reasoned, Maria was under way too much stress—which couldn't be good for her or for the baby. Somehow he had to convince the lady to marry him if not for their sakes, then for the baby's sake. ''I think it's pretty obvious what we need to do first.''

''You mean we should get married.''

Ignoring the fact that she'd made the idea sound as about appealing as having a tooth pulled, he said, ''That's right. And I think the sooner we do, the better.''

''I knew that's what you'd say,'' she accused and pulled away from him. ''It's the reason I didn't tell you about the baby in the first place. Because I knew the moment you found out you'd start pressuring me to marry you.''

''I didn't realize that you'd find the idea of marrying me to be a fate worse than death,'' he countered, his ego smarting.

''You know that's not what I meant.''

''Then why don't you explain what you *did* mean?''

She sat down on the hearth in front of the fireplace and clasped her hands together. After a moment, she looked up at him. ''I can't imagine anything more wonderful than being married to you. And I think the woman who's your wife will be a lucky lady.''

Feeling somewhat mollified and also relieved, Steven stooped down before her and captured her hands. ''I'm the lucky one,'' he told her and smiled. ''Not only am I getting you for a wife, but a baby, too.''

Maria pulled her fingers free and stood. She moved to the other end of the hearth. ''I wasn't talking about me, Steven.''

''I was,'' he informed her. He shoved up to his feet and followed her to the opposite end of the hearth. This time, he moved in, crowded her space. ''There's only one woman I plan on marrying, Maria Barone, and that's *you.*''

She shook her head. ''We can't. Think of what it will do to our families, of the problems it will create.''

''We'll deal with our families. And we'll handle any problems that come up,'' he insisted. ''The important thing is that we'll be together. I love you. I don't want to sneak around to see you and keep our relationship a secret. I never did.''

''I know.''

''Then you should also know that I want to be able

to wake up with you in the morning and go to sleep with you in my arms every night. I want to make a dozen more babies with you. I want to grow old and gray with you, Maria Barone. Marry me," he pleaded.

"Steven, don't," she cried and started to move away.

He blocked her path. Capturing her hands in his own, he looked down into those big doe eyes. "Marry me. Say you'll be my wife."

"Oh, Steven," she sobbed and pulled her hands free. "Why won't you listen? Why won't you even try to understand? A marriage between us would never work."

"How do you know it won't work unless we try?" he demanded, exasperation making his voice harsher than he intended.

"Because I know. Marriage isn't the answer."

"As far as I'm concerned, marriage is the *only* answer," he spit out the words.

"Don't be obtuse."

How in the devil could someone so small be so stubborn, he wondered. Maybe the cavemen had had the right idea, he fumed. Because right now he was sorely tempted to toss Maria over his shoulder, drag her off somewhere and make love to her until she agreed to marry him. Surprised by the primal feelings she aroused in him, he swiped a hand down his face. *Right, Conti. You go ahead and try that stunt and Maria will cut you off at the knees.*

"You know very well what I'm talking about. Our families hate each other."

"That's their problem. Not ours."

Maria stared at him as though he'd grown two heads. "Are you going to stand there and tell me that the bitter history between the Barones and Contis doesn't matter?"

"It doesn't matter. Not to me and you. The feud between our families has nothing to do with us."

"How can you say that—especially with everything that's going on right now?"

"Easily," Steven said, although he knew it was much more complicated than he cared to admit at the moment. "If our families want to keep the feud going, let them. We don't have to be a part of it."

"No? What about the fact that your family suspects my cousin Derrick of kidnapping your sister?" And before he could respond, she continued. "What if they're right? What if Derrick is the one responsible? Can you honestly say that it doesn't affect us?"

Steven clenched his hands into fists at his sides. Acid churned in his stomach at the reminder of his sister Bianca's abduction. Unlike Maria, who had a large brood of siblings, he had only his younger sister. When he'd first received word that both she and Derrick Barone had been kidnapped, he'd alternated between panic and fury. He'd turned over every stone and then some in his effort to locate them. And once private detective Ethan Mallory had zeroed in on Derrick Barone as a suspect in the kidnapping instead of a victim, Steven had vowed to find the bastard and slit his throat if he had harmed a single hair on Bianca's head. Not even the FBI's threat to charge him with obstruction had made him ease up on his search to find his sister. But when Ethan, too, had insisted he was getting in the way and hurting the investigation instead of helping, he had finally admitted that he needed to back off. It hadn't been easy—not when he was going crazy with worry over his missing sister. Finally, he had done as Ethan requested. He'd backed off and let the detective and the FBI do their jobs. Unable to do anything more to help Bianca, he had resumed his search for Maria, which he'd abandoned upon news of the kidnapping. But even locating Maria and being here with her now hadn't eased his worries about his sister. Nothing would until he knew that Bianca was safe.

"It's obvious from your expression that you know I'm right."

"What I know is that if Derrick is the one responsible for Bianca's kidnapping and he's harmed her in any way, he'll have to answer to me."

"You see?" Maria pointed out, her voice filled with despair. "It's started already. What possible chance would we have together when there's so much hate between our families?"

Cursing his own temper, Steven struggled to rein in his emotions and reminded himself that Mallory would find his sister. Right now, Maria and their baby had to be his primary concern. "We can *make* it work. I know we can."

"Be realistic, Steven. There are simply too many things against us. A marriage between us would be a disaster."

"You're wrong," he insisted. "We love each other. We can make this work. I know we can."

Maria shook her head, and the motion sent his temper spiking again.

"I can't believe you're willing to throw away what we have all because of some stupid old feud that has nothing to do with us."

"It's not just the feud," she countered. "Look at everything that's happened to my family just since we started seeing each other."

"What are you talking about?"

"I'm talking about all the things that have gone wrong

this past year beginning with that fiasco in February with the launch of the new passionfruit flavor for Baronessa Gelati. And then there was the fire at our plant. Then Derrick and Bianca were kidnapped. And now, now Derrick's been accused of kidnapping your sister.''

''And your point is?'' he asked, not liking at all the direction in which she was heading.

''The point is there's more bitterness between our families now than ever.''

''Maybe there wouldn't be if your family hadn't accused mine of sabotage,'' Steven defended. While he had never shared in his family's dislike of the Barones or bought into what he considered a silly feud, he knew his family well enough to know that they would never resort to something that was both illegal and immoral. And the sabotage and fire at the Barone's business were both.

''Can you blame them?'' Maria countered. ''Look at all the tragedies my family has suffered because of the Conti curse.''

Steven swore at the mention of the curse. ''There is no curse.''

''Try telling that to your Aunt Lucia since she's the one responsible for putting the curse on my family in the first place.''

Gritting his teeth, Steven said, ''That so-called curse was nothing more than the foolish rantings of a broken-hearted and angry teenage girl nearly seventy years ago. It isn't real. There is no curse.''

''Why? Because you say it doesn't exist? Well, I've got news for you, Steven Conti. Just because you don't believe in the curse doesn't mean it's not real. It is real. I know it is.''

''Maria, love, listen to yourself,'' Steven reasoned. He

searched to find the right words to allay her fears. He didn't believe in the Conti curse, never had, never would. As far as he was concerned the curse was exactly what he'd claimed—the lashing out of a brokenhearted teenager who'd been jilted. Yet over the years the stories about the curse had taken on mythic proportions. Well, he'd be damned if he was going to let some crazy superstition stand in the way of his and Maria's future. "Think, Maria. Think. You're one of the smartest women I know. Surely you can see that all this talk about a curse is… It's absurd."

"Maybe to you. But not to me. And not to my family. The curse exists, Steven. We Barones have been on the receiving end of it for far too long to pretend otherwise."

Steven realized that Maria's heightened emotional state due to her pregnancy might allow her to buy into the idea of the curse more easily now than she might have under other circumstances. But he had enough obstacles to overcome in order to convince Maria to marry him. He simply couldn't allow that blasted curse to be one of them. "I'm not saying your fears aren't real. I know they are. But the Maria I know and love would never let fear dictate how she lives her life."

"It's not only my life I have to consider now. It's the baby's life, too."

Steven moved closer, stared down into her eyes. "Don't you know that I'd never let anything or anyone harm you or our baby?"

"I know *you* wouldn't. But there are some things that are beyond even your control."

"So you're willing to throw away our future and our child's future on the basis of an old wives' tale about a curse," he accused, frustration eating at him.

"I told you. It's not just the curse that's the problem. It's our families. They're enemies. And with the exception of my cousin Karen, no one has any idea that we've been seeing each other, let alone that I'm pregnant. Can you imagine how my family is going to feel when I tell them that you're the baby's father?"

They'd be as shocked as his family would be, he admitted in silence. "So, it will come as a surprise. But once they realize how we feel about each other, they'll come around."

"They'll think I betrayed them."

Her words cut through him like a knife. Worse, he had a sick feeling in his stomach that it wasn't just her family Maria was talking about. "Is that what you think, too? Do you think you've betrayed your family by being with me?"

"That's not what I said."

"No, you claimed you won't marry me because of our families and because of the curse. But maybe the real reason you're putting up such a fuss is because you've had second thoughts about being involved with me. After all, I am a Conti."

"What's that supposed to mean?" she asked.

"It means that maybe you're wondering if your family was right about us evil Contis. That maybe you too think we're behind all the problems your family's had this year." Gritting his teeth, he accused, "Maybe you think that *I* had something to do with the sabotage and the fire."

"I don't believe any such thing."

"Are you sure?" Steven pressed, temper and hurt driving him.

"I'm not even going to dignify that with an answer."

When she started to move past him, Steven stepped

in front of her, blocking her path. "Prove it. Prove you don't believe I'm the enemy, that you don't regret what we've shared."

Maria narrowed her eyes. "How?"

"Marry me. Right now," he said, not wanting to give her any more time to think about all the reasons they shouldn't be together.

"Now? You expect me to marry you right this minute?"

"Yes."

"That's crazy. We couldn't get married today, even if we wanted to."

"Sure we could," he insisted. "All we have to do is find a justice of the peace. I'm sure there's at least one somewhere in Silver Valley."

"But what about our families?"

"We'll go back to Boston and tell them together. After we're married," he informed her.

"No. No, we can't do that," she said with a shake of her head. "We couldn't spring this on them like that. I can't even imagine how they'd react."

"Hopefully, they'll offer us their congratulations."

She shot him a reproachful look. "You know they won't."

"They might surprise you, Maria. Your family loves you, and my family loves me. They'll want us to be happy. Besides, my mother's been making noises about wanting grandchildren. She's been on me to get married for years."

"I doubt she had me in mind."

"Maybe not. But she'll get used to the idea," Steven assured her. "They all will."

"Including your aunt Lucia?"

"She'll come around," Steven told her and hoped he was right.

"She hates anyone named Barone. You can't honestly believe that she'll ever accept me as your wife."

"If she wants to remain a part of my life and our baby's life, she'll accept you," Steven told her. But he knew Maria was probably right. His aunt Lucia wasn't likely to accept their union. As much as he loved the older woman, he wasn't blind to her faults—the biggest of which was her all-consuming hatred of the Barones. Unfortunately, Lucia Conti had spent nearly seventy years nurturing that hatred. He'd come to the conclusion long ago that his aunt had chosen to close herself off to any chance of ever loving again and had opted instead to make him and his sister her surrogate children. Sad as it was to admit, he suspected that he and Bianca had filled the void of a husband and children in his aunt's life. Aside from them and the restaurant, her only passion in life was her hatred of the Barones. As much as he would hate to lose his beloved aunt in his life, he would hate even more to live his life without Maria and their baby.

"Does the same hold true for your parents and sister?" Maria asked. "If they refuse to accept me as your wife, are you going to shut them out of your life, too?"

"If that's what it takes for us to be together, then yes, I will," he told her without hesitation. And he meant it. While he hoped it would never come down to having to choose between his family and Maria, he would do so if necessary.

And it would be Maria that he'd choose. Maria and their baby. "So what do you say? Will you marry me?"

Three

———

"All you have to do is say yes," Steven urged her. He squeezed her fingers, implored her with those piercing blue eyes. "Say yes and we'll go right now and find ourselves a justice of the peace to marry us. Then we'll go back to Boston and break the news to our families. Maybe they'll be happy about it, and maybe they won't. However they decide to handle things will be up to them. The important thing is that you and I will be together—together with our baby."

Maria stared at Steven. He made it all sound so simple, so easy. She loved him and wanted desperately to say yes and become his wife. But even if by some miracle she could persuade her family to accept a marriage between herself and Steven, she didn't believe the Contis would ever condone such a union. And what about the curse? Perhaps Steven was right and it was nothing more than a foolish superstition fueled by overactive imaginations. But what if it wasn't?

No matter how much she might want to be with Steven, she couldn't ignore the curse. It was the main reason she'd retreated to Montana in the first place. While she had fretted over how to tell her family and Steven about the baby, she hadn't feared them. What she had feared was the Conti curse. And she *still* feared it.

"I'm sorry, Steven," she said and pulled her hands free. She stepped back, needing some space from him, needing to be strong and walk away from him when she wanted to lose herself in his embrace. "I can't marry you."

"Can't or won't?"

She heard the frustration in his voice, read it on his face and empathized with him. She was experiencing some frustration of her own. But it couldn't be helped. "Does it really matter? Either way, the answer has to be no. I'm sorry."

"Maria—"

"Please. This isn't easy for me. Don't make things any harder than they already are."

"Is that what I'm doing, Maria? Making things hard for you? Making you miserable? Funny, I thought suggesting that we get married and plan a future together with our baby would have had just the opposite effect. I thought telling you how much I love you and want to spend the rest of my life with you would make you happy."

"It did. It does," Maria told him.

"Then we—"

"No," Maria said, refusing to let him continue. She sighed. "I'm not going to play word games with you. My decision's made and I'm not changing my mind.

Please accept it. I don't want to argue with you about this anymore.''

''It certainly sounds like you know what you don't want. You don't want to play word games. You don't want to argue and you don't want to marry me,'' he repeated, ticking off the items on his fingertips. ''Tell me, Maria. Do you know what it is you do want?''

''Yes. I want you to leave. I want you to go back to Boston and forget about me. Forget about us.''

His mouth tightened. ''What about the baby? Am I supposed to forget that the child you're carrying is mine, too?'' he asked, his voice deathly soft, his eyes wintry.

Maria swallowed. ''It would be better for everyone concerned if you did. I told you, no one except my cousin Karen knows about our involvement. So no one has to know that you're the baby's father.''

''I know,'' he all but growled the words. ''That's my child you're carrying and I'll be damned if I'll pretend it isn't. I can't believe that you'd ask me to.''

''Steven, please. What I meant—''

''I know exactly what you meant. You'd just as soon no one knew that you were ever involved with me, let alone that you're pregnant with my baby.''

''Not for the reasons you think.'' Realizing how deeply she'd hurt him, she reached out to touch him.

''Don't,'' he said, staying her hand. He whipped around, giving her his back. But not before Maria had seen the rage and the pain washing across his features. Tension emanated from him—in the stiff line of his spine as he strode to the end of the hearth and put more distance between them. It was there in the way he clenched his fists at his sides.

Maria didn't know what to say, how to ease the hurt her poor attempt to reason with him had caused. ''I'm sorry," she finally said. "I'm not trying to be cruel. The last thing I want to do is hurt you."

"Sure could have fooled me."

"Steven, will you at least look at me," she pleaded, hoping she could make him understand.

But when he turned around, the bitterness she'd heard in his voice was no match for the bitterness in his expression. In all the time she'd known Steven, in all the hours she'd spent in his company, she couldn't ever recall seeing him look so cold, so forbidding. Not even when she'd refused to go public with their relationship had he looked at her with such disdain. Having him look at her that way now cut her to the quick. But then, she'd just tossed his offer of marriage back in his face. Not only that, she'd asked him to forget that he was the father of the baby she was carrying. That her reasons for doing so had been to protect their baby didn't make her asking him to deny his rights as a father any more palatable. She could hardly blame him for being angry. He had every right to be, she reasoned. But what choice did she have? "I'm sorry," she told him again and wished that the words didn't sound quite so empty.

"So am I," he replied.

"I realize I'm expecting a lot by asking you to walk away from the baby."

"You're damn right about that."

Ignoring his sarcasm, she continued, "But I'm asking you anyway. I truly believe it's what's best for everyone concerned—even if it doesn't seem that way to you right now." When he remained silent and simply continued to look at her with those cold eyes, she pressed on, "You have my word that I'll take good care of our baby and I'll be the very best mother I can. And I promise you that someday I'll tell our child the truth about you. He or she will know how much you wanted them. I'll understand if you hate me for asking you to do this. But I'm asking you anyway. No, I'm begging you. Please just walk out that door and forget about me. Forget about the baby. Forget everything that's happened between us this past year.''

"It might be easier to cut out my heart," he said with disdain.

Maria's heart ached at his words because they described her own feelings. Forgetting him would be like forgetting a part of herself. But she had to remain strong—for all their sakes. "If you feel anything at all for me…if you ever felt anything for me, you'll do this for me.''

His expression grew even more forbidding. "I love you—more than I ever imagined I could love another human being. But not even for you will I turn my back on my child.''

"Steven—''

"That's *my* child you're carrying, Maria. *My* child. No way do I intend to ignore that fact. And there is no way I'm going back to Boston without you.''

While in her heart she knew he had every right to feel as he did, she had to think of her baby. Steven was a formidable man. She had to be equally formidable. "You don't have a choice," she challenged, knowing even as she made the statement that it was a lie. "You can't force me to go back to Boston with you. And you certainly can't force me to marry you.''

"You're right. I can't force you to come with me and I certainly can't force you to marry me. But it works both ways, angel face. You can't force me to leave Montana. And whether we're married or not, I've got parental rights where that baby you're carrying is concerned—rights that I have no intention of giving up.''

Maria placed a protective hand over her swollen stomach. He was right. She knew he was right. Suddenly she had images of facing Steven in a courtroom and him demanding custody of their baby. ''You would actually fight me for custody?'' she asked, hating the quiver that snuck into her voice.

His expression softened somewhat. So did his voice as he said, ''I'm not some kind of monster, Maria. I wouldn't do that to you or to our child. But I'm not going to walk away from the two of you either. I want you and our baby.''

''Steven—''

''I love you. I know you're afraid our being together will create problems, but our families might surprise us. They could actually be happy for us once we tell them about the baby.''

''They'll be furious. The news will destroy them,'' Maria assured him. She could already imagine the look of shock and betrayal on her parents' faces. She didn't even want to think about how the Contis would take the news. ''Our families will disown us.''

''You could be right. But you could also be wrong. We'll never know unless we tell them.''

''And if I'm right?''

''Then the loss will be theirs. Maria, don't you see? We owe ourselves and our baby this chance. Whatever they do, we can handle it as long as we face this together. I'll willing to take that risk.''

But was she? She thought again of the curse, thought of a pregnant Angelica Barone who'd lost her baby on Valentine's Day. What if she listened to Steven and something happened to her baby? ''I'm not.''

"Maria," he began and started to move toward her.

Maria shook her head. "Please, Steven, I'm very tired. I'd appreciate it if you'd go now."

He hesitated, and for a moment Maria thought he was going to refuse her.

Instead he said, "All right. I'll go but only as far as my hotel." He hooked a lock of hair behind her ear and pressed a featherlight kiss to her lips. "I love you and I'm not giving up on us."

"There can be no us," she told him firmly. "Goodbye, Steven. I'll let you see yourself out." And with the taste of him still on her lips and her heart heavy with the weight of her decision, she exited the room.

Steven bit back the urge to follow her. Allowing Maria to walk away from him had been among the most difficult things he'd ever done, Steven admitted. Once she'd disappeared down the corridor and up the stairs, he drew in a deep breath, then released it. The initial anger he'd experienced upon her refusal to marry him had dissolved almost as quickly as it had come when he'd realized how stressed out Maria was. While the pang of her rejection still lingered, his own feelings took a back seat to his concern for Maria.

He was worried about her. Seriously worried. She'd looked as fragile as glass standing there beside the fireplace staring up at him out of troubled dark eyes in a face that seemed to grow paler by the second. The faint shadows beneath those eyes that he'd noted earlier had deepened and stood out like faint bruises. A closer inspection of her face had revealed taut lines of strain that had formed tiny creases along her forehead. And that strain had been mirrored in the way she'd clasped and unclasped her hands repeatedly. Maria was stressed to the max. Not that she'd ever admit such a thing. She wouldn't. She'd be more inclined to push herself until she dropped—which would be bad for both her and the baby.

So he had backed off instead. It hadn't been easy. Stubbornness and determination were traits the two of them had in common. But it had been necessary, he reasoned. He might as well leave for now, he decided and headed down the same corridor Maria had taken. It was only a temporary retreat, he told himself as he made his way toward the foyer. After all, he'd meant what he'd told Maria. He had no intention of going back to Boston without her. But first he would need to come up with a plan to help her get past her paranoia about the curse and her fears of their families' reaction to their news. And it would have to be a plan that wouldn't put her under any further stress.

Reaching the alcove near the front door where his jacket hung on the coatrack, he was debating whether to search out the Calderones to say his goodbyes or simply call them later, when a smiling Magdalene Calderone turned the corner and spied him.

"Ah, Steven, there you are. I was just on my way to get you and Maria. The coffee and hot chocolate are ready. And Louis has convinced me that we should all sample those cinnamon rolls."

"Actually, Magdalene, I think I'll pass on the coffee and rolls for now. But I hope you'll give me a rain check."

Her smile disappeared. "You are leaving us already? But where is Maria?" she asked, glancing in the direction from which he'd come.

"She went upstairs to rest. So I thought I'd go back to my hotel for now."

"Maria is not feeling well?" she asked, concern lacing her accented voice.

"She said she was tired and to be honest, she looked tired. But I'm afraid our conversation upset her." He hesitated a moment, then explained, "As you've probably guessed, I didn't know about the baby."

"Yes, I suspected as much."

"I suppose I probably should have put two and two together, and in hindsight I don't know how I could have missed all the signs." Now that he thought about it, he remembered how tired and under the weather Maria had been those last few times that they'd been together. Idiot that he was, he'd attributed it to the stress of her job and keeping their affair a secret from her family. "But somehow I *did* manage to miss them. I never suspected she was pregnant."

"Obviously."

Steven grimaced, thought he detected a note of censure in her tone. Although he'd only just met Magdalene Calderone and he knew it shouldn't, her opinion of him mattered.

"Well, now that you know about the baby, what do you intend to do?"

Considering the circumstances, her question was probably the equivalent of having a shotgun pointed at him by the wronged woman's family, Steven thought with amusement. The analogy made him realize how such a scenario would certainly answer his problem of getting Maria to marry him.

Magdalene narrowed her eyes. "You find my question amusing?"

"No," Steven told her, sobering at once.

"So you have not answered me. Maria is expecting your baby. What do you intend to do about it?"

Steven couldn't help but admire her bluntness. So he was equally direct as he answered, "I intend to marry her."

"A marriage entered into out of duty only will not make either of you happy," she cautioned.

"It won't be a marriage of duty. I love Maria and I want her to be my wife."

Magdalene's expression brightened immediately. She smiled up at him. "I knew I was right about you. You are a good man, Steven Conti of Boston. You will make Maria happy and be a good husband to her and a good father to the little one she carries. Yes?"

"Yes," he promised. And he fully intended to keep that promise.

She tipped her head, stared at him closely. "So why instead of joy in your eyes do I see the look of a man going to battle?"

The lady was sharp, Steven realized. "It's a long and complicated story," he told her.

"I like long, complicated stories."

If she did, he had a real winner to tell her, Steven thought. "How much do you know about Maria's family?"

"Other than the fact that she has a large family and that Maria loves them very much, most of what I know about them I've learned from Karen. She told us how her father, Timothy Rawlins, bless his soul, was actually Luke Barone. He'd been kidnapped as a child and renamed Timothy Rawlins. I also know that Maria and her family have been very good to Karen. She loves them— particularly Maria—very much."

"Has either Maria or Karen said anything to you about the Conti curse?"

Magdalene's dark eyes widened. "The Conti curse? There is a curse?"

"So they tell me."

Magdalene made the sign of the cross, then clasped her hands against her breast.

Steven frowned. "Personally, I don't believe in such things. I think it's nothing more than old Sicilian superstitions and a lot of overactive imaginations at work. Unfortunately, I haven't been able to convince Maria of that."

"You are a tall one, Steven, and I'm getting a crick in my neck looking up at you. I think you should come into the kitchen and have that coffee after all. Then you can tell me all about this Conti curse."

From his seat at the kitchen table, Steven glanced over to the bright orange and cream draped window. Outside the sun had already set, early as it does in the winter months. But a light snow was falling and he could see the soft blanket of white dusting the pines. Sitting there with the down-to-earth Calderones in the warm, cozy room filled with the aroma of cinnamon and coffee, Boston, the Conti curse and the problems between his and Maria's families seemed a million miles away.

The last thing he'd felt like doing was rehashing the details of the Conti/Barone feud. But if he were going to be successful in convincing Maria to marry him and return to Boston, he needed the Calderones' help. And in order to get their help, they'd need to understand what he was up against.

Magdalene refilled the coffee cup in front of Louis and topped off Steven's cup, then returned the glass pot to the counter. "And even after all this time your two families still are sworn enemies?" she asked.

"Yes," Steven replied. "If a Barone is walking down the street and he sees a Conti on the same block, he'll cross the street to avoid being near him. And when they do come face-to-face, it can get ugly."

"Obviously you and Maria didn't have that problem," Magdalene pointed out as she resumed her seat at the table.

A smile tugged at Steven's lips at the memory. "Since I'm not involved in my family's restaurant business and travel a lot for my own firm, I don't often cross paths with members of the Barone family or them with me. So when Maria and I met, she didn't realize I was a Conti and I didn't know she was a Barone. But even if I had known who she was, it wouldn't have stopped me from pursuing her. I wanted her the moment I set eyes on her," he admitted honestly.

"And Maria? How did she feel when she discovered who you were?" Magdalene asked him.

"Let's just say she's very loyal to her family," he answered, remembering Maria's dismay when she'd learned his identity. "It took some convincing on my part to get her to see me again. Fortunately, I did."

"And the two of you fell in love, but your families remain enemies," Magdalene surmised. "It is almost like *Romeo and Juliet.*"

Steven hadn't thought of his and Maria's relationship in quite those terms before, he realized. But he could understand how Magdalene had drawn such an analogy since their situation presented a similar problem with their families. Only he had no intention of their love affair coming to the same tragic end as the famed Shakespearean lovers.

"When Karen told us that her cousin Maria was pregnant and under a lot of strain and needed to get away for a while, we had no idea what she was facing," Magdalene said. "And since Maria never mentioned her baby's father, we thought there might have been some sort of a lovers' quarrel between the two of you. But we never dreamed it was anything so complicated."

"It is small wonder that Maria has seemed so unhappy," Louis said. "All this feuding between your families, it cannot have made things easy for her," he added. "For you, either, I imagine."

"It's been hardest on Maria," Steven told him. "Other than Karen, no one else in her family knows about us."

"And your family?" Louis asked.

Steven shook his head. "They don't know either. I wanted to go public with our relationship months ago, but Maria wanted to wait. There were some sabotage problems at Baronessa and because of the years of animosity, suspicion fell on my family. Maria felt the timing was all wrong and wanted us to wait until things settled down, and I foolishly agreed. I should have just insisted then that we come clean and tell our families about us."

"Perhaps. But knowing Maria, whether you insisted or not, if she was determined to keep your relationship a secret, I doubt that you would have been able to change her mind," Magdalene offered.

Steven suspected the comment was meant to ease his conscience, but he found it to be of little comfort. "Well, it won't be a secret much longer," Steven informed them.

"No, it won't," Magdalene agreed.

"The baby is due in a little over two months and her family doesn't even know she's pregnant," he said, unable to keep the frustration from his voice. "And I'm sure she's worrying herself sick over how they're going to take the news that a Conti is the baby's father.''

"Given all that you have told us about the history of your two families, her concern is justified, don't you think?'' Magdalene asked.

"Yes,'' Steven admitted. "But I hate knowing what all this stress is doing to her.'' He pushed aside his coffee cup, leaned forward. "I love Maria and I intend to marry her no matter what either of our families wants.''

"Good for you,'' Louis told him.

Magdalene beamed like a proud mama.

"But if I'm going to be successful, I'll need your help.''

"You have it,'' Magdalene assured him. She glanced toward her husband and Steven witnessed the silent question that passed between them.

Nodding his assent, Louis placed his hand atop his wife's. Then he brought his gaze back to Steven's. "Tell us what it is you want us to do.''

Four

___

"**O**h those look absolutely wonderful," Magdalene said several afternoons later as Maria transferred the tray of Italian fig cookies from the cookie sheet onto the wax paper lining the countertop.

"They taste even better," Maria informed her. Reaching for the bowl of green-colored icing she'd prepared, she began to drizzle the confectioner's sugar, milk and anise-flavored topping over the still warm cookies. The traditional Italian cookies had always been a favorite of hers and were one of the most popular items at Baronessa. No small wonder, she thought with pleasure, since the recipe used was the same one that had been handed down by her great-great-grandmother. While preparing the treat for Silver Valley's church Christmas Bazaar had helped to keep her busy, it had also made her homesick for her family.

"Do you want me to put those little sprinkles on top

as you ice them?'' Magdalene asked, motioning to the bowl of multicolored candy sprinkles that Maria had placed at the end of the counter.

"Please. That way the sprinkles will harden with the icing,'' Maria told her. She moved down the line of cookies and continued to drizzle the sweet topping with practiced ease. When she'd been a young girl, icing the fig cookies had been one of the first jobs that her grandmother had assigned her at Baronessa, Maria recalled fondly. Thoughts of her grandmother set off another pang of loneliness. If her grandmother were still alive, what would she say about Steven and the baby? Would she be disappointed in her? Would she feel betrayed?

Trying to shake off the disturbing thoughts, Maria glanced up from her task and went still at the sight of Steven walking past the kitchen window, his arms loaded with fresh-cut firewood.

"Uh, Maria, *pequeña,* I think you may have put a bit too much icing on that one.''

Maria dragged her attention from the window to the fig cookie she'd been icing and groaned. Instead of a few swirls of green icing across the top of the inch-long cookie, the thing was a solid lump of green. Chastising herself silently, Maria slapped the spoon back into the bowl. Then she began wiping up some of the excess icing that had overflowed onto the wax paper and was oozing along the edges of the other cookies.

Magdalene chuckled. "Why don't you just leave it. I'm sure Louis and Steven will be happy to eat any of our mess-ups.''

Maria scowled at Magdalene's remark. In the five days since she'd turned down Steven's proposal and had refused to return with him to Boston, he had been back to the Calderones' each day. Although he'd made no further mention of marriage and hadn't pressured her again to tell their families about the baby, he had somehow managed to befriend the Calderones and weave himself into their daily lives. She didn't like it. She didn't like it at all, she admitted. Not for one minute was she buying Steven's "taking a break" act. Using a spatula, she lifted the overiced cookie from the wax paper and plopped it onto a plate.

"You know, perhaps we should mess up a few more of these," Magdalene said with a sly smile. "That way we can have them tonight for dessert."

"I thought you said you were putting Louis on a diet and had outlawed desserts," Maria reminded her.

Magdalene waved aside the objection and said, "I *am* putting him on a diet. But since we're having a guest for dinner, we should at least offer some type of dessert. Besides, we both know what a sweet tooth my Louis has. I can hardly expect him to resist these cookies," Magdalene continued as she scooped up a fingerful of icing and licked it.

"What guest?" Maria asked.

"Steven," Magdalene replied innocently. She picked up her dish of sprinkles. "The other tray of cookies will be ready soon. Don't you wish to finish icing the rest of these cookies while they are still warm?"

Maria snatched up her bowl of icing. "Just because Steven is…because he and I…" She huffed out a breath and started over. "You didn't have to invite Steven to dinner on my account," she told the other woman as she whipped the remaining frosting in the dish with a vengeance, then began drizzling it over the rows of cookies.

"I didn't invite him. Louis did."

"Well, Louis shouldn't have felt obligated to invite him for my sake."

"Louis did not invite him because of you," Magdalene informed her. "It was to repay him for helping mend the fences."

"Oh," Maria said and nearly cringed at how inane she had sounded.

"Steven is a good man, *pequeña,* and he loves you."

"I know." And she loved him. Which made the situation all the more painful. But that didn't mean that the two of them should be together—not when so many of the people they loved stood to be hurt by their relationship.

"Then why not give him a chance?"

"You know why," Maria told her, not wanting to rehash her reasons for refusing Steven's proposal. Halfheartedly she iced another row of cookies and hoped Magdalene would just let the subject drop.

"You are referring to this feud between your families."

Maria nodded. "What chance would we have when our being together would tear our families apart?" And she and Steven would probably end up hating each other. She didn't think she could bear having Steven grow to hate her and blame her for the loss of his family. What kind of life would that be for them? For their baby?

"I think you underestimate yourself and Steven, Maria. You are a strong and brave young woman, and from what I have learned of Steven, he is equal to the task. Why not at least try?"

"Because I'm afraid," Maria admitted. She looked up from the countertop filled with cookies and met Magdalene's eyes. "I'm afraid of what might happen to my baby."

Magdalene looked at her closely for a moment and

then her eyes widened with understanding. "The Conti curse," she whispered.

"Yes," Maria said and felt the prickle of tears behind her eyelids. "I know it sounds foolish and I don't expect you to understand, but I just can't risk it."

"Ah, *mi pobre pequeña.*" Magdalene put down the dish of sprinkles, took the bowl of icing from Maria, set it aside and opened her arms. She hugged Maria close and stroked her hair as though she were a child.

Suddenly it all seemed too much and Maria began to sob.

"There, there," Magdalene comforted, patting her back. "Go ahead and have yourself a good cry. You'll feel better."

After a few moments, Maria regained control of herself. She stepped back and swiped her eyes and damp cheeks with the hem of her apron. "I'm sorry. I don't know why I'm being such a ninny," Maria told her.

"No need to be sorry. And you are no ninny," Magdalene assured her. "I told you, you are a very brave young woman."

"Who cries for no good reason."

"You have many reasons to cry," Magdalene said seriously. "But you have more reasons to smile—that little one you are carrying," she continued, shifting her gaze to Maria's belly. "And a man who loves you very much."

"I know," she said, feeling ashamed to have indulged in self-pity even for a moment.

"Love can be a powerful weapon, Maria. Even more powerful than a curse."

The oven buzzer sounded, saving her from having to respond. She seized on the opportunity to change the subject. "Goodness, I must be losing my touch," she declared as she grabbed the oven mitts and headed for the oven. "I used to be able to ice an entire batch of cookies and have time for a cup of coffee before the next batch was ready. Can you spread out a couple of sheets of wax paper on the other counter?"

Magdalene gave her a knowing look, but picked up the roll of wax paper and measured out several sheets to cover the countertops. "The red icing for these?" she asked.

"Please," Maria told her as she quickly transferred the hot cookies onto the wax paper and placed the cookie sheet out of harm's way. "Thanks," she said and took the bowl of icing from Magdalene.

"You know Kirsten Van Dych is forever bragging that those fancy chocolate candies she donates for the bazaar are made from authentic Belgian recipes that have been in her family for years," Magdalene said as she resumed her sprinkling duties. "Just wait until I tell her that these cookies were made from an authentic Italian recipe that is used at Baronessa's."

"Actually this particular recipe has been in the Barone family for more than a century," Maria informed her. Within minutes, they were once again chatting about the upcoming Christmas Bazaar and life in Silver Valley, abandoning further talk about the Conti curse and Steven.

"So when do you think you'll be coming to Boston to visit Karen?" Steven asked the Calderones while seated at the dinner table with them that evening.

"I'm not sure," Magdalene responded. "Definitely not until after the New Year. Or perhaps sometime in February. Maybe around the time when your and Maria's baby is due."

"I...Maria and I," Steven amended, "We would love to have you there for the baby's birth. Wouldn't we, Maria?" he asked, doing his best to draw her into the conversation.

"It would mean a great deal to me if you could be with me when the baby's born," Maria said, directing her remarks to the Calderones. "But I've been thinking about having the baby here in Silver Valley. I realize it's an imposition and—"

"Nonsense," Magdalene said. "You are welcome to stay here as long as you like. And Louis and I would love for your and Steven's little one to be born here."

"Magdalene is right," Louis added, his voice deep and the hint of his Spanish heritage marking his speech. "You are welcome to stay with us as long as you like. But the arrival of a baby is a time for family. Are you sure you do not wish to be closer to your own family for such an important event?"

Steven shot Louis a silent look of thanks. "Louis is right. Once we tell our families about the baby, they'll all be pretty anxious for the arrival. It would probably be easier for everyone to be there if the baby's born in Boston."

Maria replied in a flat voice, "That's assuming my family's still speaking to me when I tell them the news."

"When *we* tell them," Steven corrected.

When Maria fell silent once again, Steven did his best to rein in his frustration. He'd never been long on patience, a fact that Ethan Mallory had pointed out to him in a less than polite manner when Steven had called the P.I. that morning demanding that the FBI bring in more help to locate his sister. Despite what his former brother-in-law believed, he had exercised an enormous amount of patience since his arrival in Silver Valley—ever since he'd realized how stressed out Maria was. But after five days of hanging out at the Calderones and trying to get Maria to relax around him so that he could ease her into the idea of marrying him, he felt no closer to his goal now than he'd been when he had arrived. How in the devil was he supposed to convince her to marry him when she barely said ten words to him and avoided him at every chance? And what was he going to do if she dug in her heels and insisted on remaining in Montana to have the baby?

Refusing to accept that as a possibility, he tried again. "Then it's settled," he told the Calderones. "Maria and I will expect you both in Boston for Valentine's Day to celebrate the baby's birth with us."

"You have a date," Magdalene replied.

"Good. And I want you to stay long enough so that I have a chance to repay your hospitality. While I can't promise a meal as sumptuous as this one, I know my way around the kitchen."

"Oh, but that is not necessary, Steven. You and Maria will be so busy with your little one," Magdalene pointed out.

"Maria's the one with the tough job. Besides dinner shouldn't be too difficult. I think I can still remember how to whip up some pasta. But if necessary, I can always order takeout from my folks' restaurant. Conti's serves the best Italian food in Boston."

At the mention of his family's place, Maria visibly stiffened. Quickly she averted her gaze and began staring at the food on her plate—but not before he'd seen the troubled look in her eyes. Steven immediately wanted to kick himself for the slip of tongue.

"Louis and I will look forward to it, then," Magdalene said, breaking the silence and some of the tension.

"But for now, why don't I get you some more of that roast?"

Steven could have kissed the other woman for the diversion. Holding up his hands, he smiled and said, "As much as I'd like to, I think I'd better pass. If I eat any more, I won't be able to move. But thank you anyway. The roast was absolutely delicious."

"I told you my Magdalene is a wonderful cook," Louis claimed proudly, a wide smile creasing his weathered face. "It is one of the reasons I married her."

"Really? I do not seem to recall any mention of my cooking skills when you asked me to marry you, Louis Calderone."

The other man's grin faded. Alarm clouded his dark eyes. "I said it was *one* of the reasons I married you, *mi amor,*" Louis replied, looking like a man who'd just found himself in the middle of a minefield. "But it was *you,* your beauty and your sweetness that I fell in love with."

Steven bit back a grin at the other man's snappy recovery and noted Magdalene's silent arch of her brow. Watching the pair, he couldn't help envy the Calderones the closeness that came from years spent as husband and wife. It made him realize just how badly he wanted that same kind of closeness for himself and Maria.

But how was he ever going to realize that dream when he could barely get Maria to look at him?

"It is true, Magdalene," Louis told his wife. "Your being such a wonderful cook was only an added bonus."

"Actually Louis was telling me just this morning how the two of you met," Steven began. "He said he was passing through Silver Valley during a festival when he saw you. And just like that," he said with a snap of his fingers, ''he fell like a ton of bricks and has been here ever since.''

''It was the weekend of the Big Sky Summer Festival,'' Magdalene explained, her expression softening with her voice. ''I had just graduated from high school and was working at Miss Ellie's Diner for the summer when Louis came.''

''I was on my way to Butte and stopped for a bite to eat. I pulled up a chair at the diner and was studying the menu when I heard the voice of an angel ask me if I wanted to hear the day's specials. I looked up and there she was. The most beautiful creature I had ever set my eyes on.''

''You ordered the special—beef steak and mashed potatoes,'' Magdalene reminded her husband.

''You could have told me the special was sawdust and I would have ordered it. It was as though I had been struck by a lightning bolt. All I could see was you.''

''He hung around for nearly three hours drinking black coffee and eating three different desserts until I got off work,'' Magdalene explained.

''I asked if I could walk you home, but you said you were meeting a girlfriend at the festival,'' Louis added.

''My friend Linda Garcia…Linda Ramos now,'' Magdalene said. ''Louis claimed he was in town for the festival and asked if we would mind if he tagged along with us. But it was a fib. He'd never planned to go to the festival at all.''

''It was only a small fib,'' he countered, never taking his eyes from his wife as the two of them retold the tale of their first meeting. ''And it got you to spend the evening with me.''

''Poor Linda, you pushed her off on that obnoxious Buck Martin,'' Magdalene accused.

"I had to do something," Louis offered in defense. "Linda's mouth—it was never still. And she has this whiny voice that hurts a body's ears, like fingernails scratching on a chalkboard."

"She has a perfectly lovely voice," Magdalene defended.

"Yes. If you like the sound of a cat wailing."

"Louis! What a thing to say!"

"It is true," Louis insisted.

"Well, maybe her voice is a little high-pitched. But she was only trying to be friendly."

"She was not the one I wanted to be friendly with. *You* were. I knew the moment I set my eyes on you that you were the girl I wanted to spend the rest of my life with." He leaned over and kissed his wife lightly on the lips.

As the pair exchanged loving looks, Steven slanted a glance over to Maria. Except for the remark about possibly remaining in Silver Valley, she had said very little all through dinner. Since he'd mentioned his family, she'd said nothing. He willed her to look at him now, to share his amusement at the other couple's love story. Finally, as though she had sensed his wishes, she lifted her gaze. Humor glinted in her brown eyes. Steven smiled and was rewarded by the tug of a grin on her lips.

Magdalene tapped her husband on his hand. "Really, Louis. We have guests. I am sure Maria and Steven are quite bored with the tale of our romance."

"Not at all," Steven assured Magdalene. "It reminds me of how I felt the first time I saw Maria."

"Steven, I doubt that Magdalene and Louis are interested in hearing how we met," Maria informed him.

"Oh, but we are. Please, tell us," Magdalene encouraged him.

Maria sat back in her chair, crossed her arms. But when no further objections were forthcoming, Steven continued, "I met Maria at the wedding of my college roommate's sister Gail."

"The groom was a Barone," Maria pointed out.

"Maria's right. Her brother Nicholas was the groom, but I didn't allow the fact that he was a Barone to stop me from attending."

"That's because you were interested in Gail's friend," Maria accused.

Encouraged by the flash of heat in her voice, Steven explained, "I'll admit the notion of becoming better acquainted with one of Gail's bridesmaids was one of the reasons I went to the wedding. But then I looked across the room and saw this gorgeous brunette with the most incredible brown eyes."

"Maria," Magdalene said.

"Yes. The minute I saw her, I forgot all about the other woman. All I could think of was that I had to meet her."

"How romantic," Magdalene said. "What did you do?"

"I asked her to dance and monopolized her time the rest of the evening. When the reception was over and the band was packing up to leave, I refused to let her out of my arms until she gave me her phone number and a kiss."

"Because you didn't know I was a Barone."

"It wouldn't have mattered if I had known," Steven informed her. "I told you who your family is didn't matter to me then. And it doesn't matter to me now." Forgetting his audience, he told Maria, "I'm not going to throw away what we have, the future we can have together with our baby, just because of some ridiculous feud and superstitious nonsense."

Maria shoved to her feet, tipping over her chair in the process. "I keep telling you it's not nonsense. And it's not your decision to make. It's mine. I'm sorry, Magdalene, Louis, but I…I… Excuse me," she cried out and then fled the room.

"Maria, wait!"

"Let her go," Magdalene said, putting a hand on his arm when he started to go after her.

"But she's upset."

"Yes. And if you go after her now and try to convince her you're right, it will only upset her more. Try to be patient."

"I have been patient and it isn't working." Steven sank back down in his seat. He shoved a hand through his hair, then let out an exasperated breath.

"But it is working. Why do you think she was so upset?"

"Huh?"

Magdalene laughed and reached out and patted his hand. "I saw Maria's face when you spoke of this other woman. She was jealous."

"She has no reason to be jealous. I haven't looked at another woman since I met her. She's the one I love. She's the woman I want to marry."

"And she feels the same way. But she's scared. She fears losing her family and she also fears for her baby's safety."

"Because of that damn curse," Steven spit out. Frustration gnawed at him, making him feel raw inside.

"Try to be a little more patient."

"I'm not sure I can. I'm running out of time, Magdalene. I spoke to the detective handling my sister's kidnapping today. Things are at a standstill and the longer she's missing, the worse the chances are that we'll get her back unharmed.'' Deciding he needed to be honest, he said, ''I need to get back to Boston, but I don't want to leave here without Maria.''

''Maybe you won't have to,'' Magdalene told him, a satisfied gleam coming into her eyes. ''I have an idea— one that could help speed things up.''

Five

Magdalene had been right. The long soak in the tub had helped her to relax, Maria thought as she exited the bathroom adjoining her bedroom. So had the Calderones' gracious acceptance of her apology for the emotional and hasty retreat she'd made from the dining room earlier that evening. Despite Magdalene's assurance that the incident was of no consequence and that they understood the pressure she was under, Maria couldn't help but be appalled by her actions.

She was the manager of a successful business. She'd dealt with hundreds of disasters since taking the helm of Baronessa Gelateria. And she'd done so calmly. Her own family swore she was not only the image of her late grandmother Angelica, but that she possessed the same cool head and decisiveness as the Baronessa's founder.

So where was that cool-headed, decisive woman now? And when had she become such an emotional wreck?

Since she'd fallen in love with Steven, the voice inside her head whispered. Maria sighed. Although he'd been gone when she'd returned downstairs and she'd been spared facing him again tonight, she was going to have to face him. She was also going to have to face their situation because of the baby. And she was going to have to do it soon.

Smoothing a hand over her protruding stomach, Maria sighed. If only she knew what to do. If only she could figure out some way for her and the baby to be with Steven without ripping their families apart. But try as she might, she didn't see any way for that to be possible. Tears pricked her eyes at the admission. Sucking in her breath, she blinked them back, refusing to give in to those feelings of despair again.

What she needed was a good night's sleep, Maria decided. Maybe in the morning she would feel better and could make the right decision for everyone concerned. After shedding her robe, she tossed it across the foot of the bed and made her way around to the side. She climbed into bed, turned out the lamp and snuggled under the covers. Closing her eyes, she tried to sleep. But for the next twenty minutes, she tossed and turned as images of Steven and her family filled her head.

Giving up, Maria sat up in bed and turned on the lamp. She looked over at the nightstand and eyed the telephone. Maybe if she could talk to Karen, she wouldn't feel so lonely and restless, she reasoned, and glanced at the clock. Ten o'clock, she noted with disappointment. Too late to call her cousin Karen outside Boston, where it'd be midnight. She and Ash were probably in bed. If not because her cousin and the sexy sheikh were still practically newlyweds, then because Karen's pregnancy no doubt exhausted her.

But thoughts of her long-lost cousin's romance and marriage with the sheikh only made her feel more depressed. While she was truly happy that things had worked out for the pair, Maria couldn't help feel a pang of envy. If only there was some way that her relationship with Steven could have a similar happy ending, she thought. But what chance did they have when both their families deemed them to be enemies from birth?

A wave of sadness rolled through her with the force of a blizzard, leaving her feeling more miserable and alone. She had to snap out of this, Maria told herself. Knowing she'd be unable to sleep, she plumped up her pillows and retrieved the thriller she'd wanted to read from the edge of the nightstand.

But ten minutes later, despite the author's skill in crafting a riveting story, Maria closed the book and set it aside. She simply couldn't appreciate the drama unfolding on the pages when the drama of her own life was foremost in her mind. She looked at the telephone again and despite the hour, she punched in Karen's phone number.

The phone was answered on the third ring. "Hello," her cousin answered.

"Hi, Karen. It's Maria."

"Maria," Karen exclaimed. "You must be psychic. I was just telling Ash that I needed to talk to you. I was planning on calling you in the morning."

"I'm sorry. I shouldn't have called so late," Maria said, wishing she hadn't made the phone call after all. "It's nothing important. Why don't I just give you a call back later."

"Maria, don't you dare hang up," Karen commanded. "I told you I wanted to talk to you, too."

Maria hesitated. "You're sure I'm not catching you and Ash at a bad time?"

"I'm positive," Karen assured her. "We were just sitting in bed arguing over names for the baby."

"We were *discussing* names for the baby," Ash called out.

Maria smiled at the sound of her new cousin-in-law's response because she knew that early in their relationship Karen had shied away from the formidable sheikh because she'd feared he would prove too controlling.

"What do you think of Ashley?" Karen asked, breaking into Maria's thoughts.

"It's a pretty name," Maria replied.

"I think so, too. And it would work whether the baby is a boy or a girl."

"Our son is not going to go through life with the name of a girl," Ash declared in the background. "It would scar him for life."

But Maria hadn't missed the note of happiness and pride in his voice. Hearing the pair banter so easily about a name for their baby made Maria long to share such moments with Steven. It also brought home the fact that any such scenario happening between herself and Steven wasn't likely.

"Men," her cousin replied a few seconds later after she'd dispatched her husband to fetch her some ice cream. "Speaking of men, is Steven still in Silver Valley?" Karen asked.

"Yes. I thought once I made it clear that I wasn't going to marry him that he'd go back to Boston. Instead he's practically become a member of the Calderone family," Maria said in frustration. "Magdalene and Louis adore him. He's here all the time, helping Louis around the ranch, charming Magdalene."

"And driving you crazy?"

"Yes. But not in the way you think. I mean, he's not pressuring me to marry him like he did that first day," she explained. "But just his being here, talking about us and the baby as though we're already a family...it's made things...more difficult," she finally said, unable to find the words to explain that Steven was making her want what she knew she couldn't have.

"Have you given any more thought about what you're going to do?"

"It's all I think about," Maria informed her.

"And?"

"And what I want to do and what I think I should do are two different things. I love Steven and I want to marry him."

"But..." Karen prompted.

"But I'm afraid of what will happen if I do."

"I seem to remember feeling the same way not very long ago. And a wise and wonderful woman told me that I shouldn't squander a chance to be with the man I loved."

Maria heard her own words being quoted back to her. "My situation is different," she defended.

"Is it? I was afraid of being rejected by Ash, that he only wanted to marry me so that he could control me. But you were the one who convinced me I'd be crazy not to take a chance. Maybe you should follow your own advice. Why not take a chance? Accept Steven's marriage proposal and then tell the family about him and the baby."

Oh, how she wished she could, Maria thought. But what if both families rejected them? And what if by her actions, her unborn baby paid the price of the curse just as her grandmother once had? "I can't," she whispered.

"It'll destroy my parents and God knows how Steven's family would react. No, I can't do it. I can't take that risk."

"People change, Maria."

"Not that much. You know how bad things have been lately. Just mention the name Conti at Baronessa and everyone's blood pressure skyrockets. Can you imagine how they'd react if I told them that Steven and I were getting married? That I was going to have a Conti's baby?"

"They might surprise you," Karen offered.

"More than likely, they'll disown me and never want to see or speak to me again." And the thought of that happening had Maria's throat growing tight with tears.

"You're going to have to tell them sooner or later," her cousin pointed out. "Everyone keeps asking where you are and when you're coming back."

Maria frowned, detecting in Karen's voice that something was wrong. "Is there a problem at Baronessa?"

"No. No new problems at least. Mimi's doing a great job holding down things at the gelateria, and the FBI is still trying to locate Derrick and Bianca Conti. But I'm afraid it's looking more and more like Derrick might be the one behind his and Bianca's kidnapping and the ransom demand."

"I was hoping we were wrong about Derrick." While she hadn't wanted to believe her cousin capable of such a thing, Maria knew that Derrick had always perceived himself as being slighted by the rest of the family. Though it wasn't true, he'd claimed his contributions to the business had been undervalued and he'd deeply resented it when he'd been put in charge of quality control at the plant and not in the corporate offices or even named as manager of Baronessa Gelateria. Maria shook her head. "I just wish I could understand why he would put our family through this."

"Whatever his reasons are, it's been hard on Emily."

"Poor Emily," Maria said, referring to Derrick's younger sister. "Do you think it would help if I called her?"

"I think she'd like that." Karen paused. "You might also want to call your parents."

Maria's heartbeat quickened. "My parents? Is something wrong? Has something happened to them?"

"No. No," Karen said quickly. "It's nothing like that."

"Then what is it?"

"Your father ran into Lucia Conti yesterday," Karen said.

Maria nearly groaned. "How bad was it?"

"Bad enough, I guess. I'm told Lucia accused the Barones of knowing where Derrick was holding Bianca. Some ugly words were exchanged."

She could hardly blame either of them, Maria thought. Her father would resent having a Barone accused of such a crime, and Lucia Conti would be frantic and angry over the disappearance of her niece. Which only brought home the impossibility of either family's acceptance of her and Steven together. She sighed. "Is that the reason you were going to call me? To tell me about my father's argument with Lucia?"

"It was one of the reasons, but not the only one. Aunt Moira and Uncle Carlo came to see me earlier this evening. That's how I found out about what happened with Lucia Conti."

"But why would my parents come to see you?" Maria began. But before Karen could answer, she said, "To find out from you where I am."

"Yes," Karen confirmed. "They're worried about you, Maria. They're not buying the line about you wanting to recharge your batteries or that you've been keeping an eye out for new outlets for Baronessa. They've figured out that you were involved with someone in Boston before you left. And they think you left because the relationship ended badly."

"Do they know it was Steven?"

"No. And I didn't tell them where you were. I explained that I'd given you my word, but I assured them that you were safe."

"Thanks," Maria said. The last thing she wanted was to have her parents show up in Silver Valley while Steven was here.

"Aunt Moira and Uncle Carlo have been very kind to me. I didn't like seeing them so worried."

"I know. And I'm sorry I've put you in this position," Maria said and truly meant it. "I'll call them tomorrow and let them know I'm all right."

"You need to come home, Maria. It's time. And you've got to tell your parents about the baby."

"I know."

"You need to do it soon."

"I will," Maria assured her. "Soon. I promise I'll do it soon. I'll come home and tell them everything."

"What are you going to do about Steven? He wants you, and from what little I know of him, he doesn't strike me as a man who gives up easily."

"You're right about that," Maria replied. "He doesn't. And now that he knows about the baby, he's even more determined for us to get married."

"Maybe you should consider it, then. After all, he is the baby's father and whether you marry him or not, he has a right to be a part of the child's life. I hate to keep throwing your words back at you, but you're the one who told me not to squander a chance to be with the man I love. Maybe you should take your own advice.''

"I'll think about it," Maria promised.

"Steven, can you help Maria put that popcorn string on that high branch near the top of the tree?" Magdalene asked two afternoons later as the four of them decorated the Calderones' Christmas tree.

"Sure," Steven said, knowing full well that the tree decorating and all the other little chores Magdalene had cooked up for them since the ill-fated dinner were an effort to throw him and Maria together. He moved behind Maria, brushed up against her back as he took the stringed popcorn and draped it on the branch.

"Thanks," Maria said, her voice a soft hush.

"No problem." Reluctant to move away, he remained close, inhaled her scent, noted the glow of her skin.

"I'd better get another string for the tree," she told him and Steven stepped back.

"Who wants eggnog?" Louis asked as he entered the den carrying a tray with Christmas mugs and a pitcher.

"I'll take a cup," Steven replied.

"Me, too," Maria said.

Dressed in a western shirt, worn jeans and boots and holding the dainty-looking tray, the older man made an amusing picture, Steven thought. But there was nothing amusing about the pride that shone in his eyes as he watched his wife pour the eggnog. Steven had never been one to envy others, but he couldn't help feeling a touch of envy now. While his life in Boston was filled with the riches of a successful career, Louis's simple life on the ranch with the woman he loved made him by far the wealthier man. Steven wanted a life with Maria. Somehow, someway, he had to convince her.

"Here you go, Steven," Magdalene said as she handed him his eggnog.

"Thanks." Taking the cup, he took a taste. "Delicious," he told Magdalene.

"It's wonderful, Magdalene," Maria said. "I hope you'll share the recipe with me. I'd love to make some for my family at Christmas."

"You have decided to go home for Christmas, then?" Magdalene asked as she refilled her husband's cup.

"I...I'm not sure," she informed her. "Maybe."

At least she was thinking about returning to Boston, Steven told himself and tried to take that as a positive sign. While he wanted to press her, insist she allow him to take her home and tell their families about the baby, he remained silent.

Maria set down her cup. "Well, I guess we better finish trimming this tree or else we'll be late for Lamaze class," Maria told Magdalene.

"Oh my heavens," Magdalene exclaimed. "Maria, *pequeña,* I forgot to tell you. I cannot go with you to the Lamaze class tonight. There is a meeting tonight for the church's holiday decorating committee and I'm the chairperson. So I have to go. I'm so sorry. I meant to tell you, but with everything going on, it slipped my mind."

"Don't worry about it," Maria said.

"But you cannot go alone. You need a partner," Magdalene insisted.

"I'll just skip class this week."

"You mustn't do that. It is important that you go. The instructor said this last trimester is the most important."

"Why don't I go with you?" Steven offered.

"An excellent idea," Magdalene said.

He knew from Maria's closed expression that she didn't feel the same way. But deciding to take the opening Magdalene had created and run with it, he said, "Since I'm the baby's father and I plan to be with you during the delivery, it only makes sense that I'm the one who goes with you."

"All right. The class is at seven-thirty in the community center next to the hospital," Maria informed him.

Steven nodded. He'd seen the hospital during his trips into Silver Valley proper. He glanced at his watch, calculated the driving time. "Because of the snowfall this afternoon, we probably should leave a little early."

"You two go ahead," Magdalene said. "Louis and I will finish up the tree."

"All right," Maria said and put her cup down on the tray. "I just need to freshen up and get my coat."

"I'll go start the car so that it's nice and warm for you when you're ready to go."

He had always had a healthy respect for women, Steven thought as the film on childbirth came to an end and the lights in the community center room came on. It was hard for him not to respect the female of the species. After all, he had grown up in a house with three of them—his mother, Aunt Lucia and his sister, Bianca. Although they were individuals with varied talents and interests, all three women were strong and intelligent. His association with other women over the years and his observation of Maria during this past year had only reinforced his belief that the term "weaker sex" was an inaccurate one. That particular belief had been reinforced after he viewed the film on natural childbirth. Of one thing he was certain—the person who had coined the ridiculous term ''weaker sex'' had obviously never seen a woman giving birth.

Were he given the option of losing an arm or having a baby, he'd probably opt to lose the arm. Steven glanced around the room at the other men in attendance. From the ashen looks on most of their faces, he wasn't the only one who'd been blown away by the ordeal on film.

''Enlightening, wasn't it?'' Maria asked from her seat beside him.

''To say the least.'' Enlightening, hell. The thing had scared him spitless. And just the idea of Maria having to go through that same experience in two months time shook him to the core.

The Lamaze class instructor, who had introduced herself as Nurse Carol, clapped her hands. ''All right, Moms, get your mats and then find a place on the floor for you and your coach.''

Somewhere in her mid-fifties, the lady was nearly six feet tall and he guessed her weight to be around a hundred sixty pounds. She didn't fit his image of a soft-spoken angel of mercy. Instead she reminded him of his third-grade teacher, Mrs. Boris—a woman he had personally believed would have made a good army drill sergeant.

Nurse Carol clapped her hands again. ''Come on, class, the fun part is over. Now it's time to get to work.''

The fun part?

The woman must have a screw loose, Steven decided, because there hadn't been anything remotely ''fun'' about the agony the woman in the film had gone through to have that baby.

''There's a spot right over there near the wall,'' Maria said, pointing to an empty section on the far side of the floor. When he didn't move, she asked, "Steven, are you all right? You look…strange."

He swiped a hand down his face. "I was just thinking about that film. If that's what a woman has to go through to have a baby, it's a miracle that I'm not an only child."

Maria chuckled. "I'm one of eight," she reminded him.

Wincing, he said, "Then your poor mother must be a saint."

Her smile faded. Worry lines creased her brow. "In a lot of ways she is a saint. I just hope I'll be half as good a mother to my baby as she's been to me."

"You're going to be a wonderful mother," he assured her.

"I hope you're right."

"I'm always right," he teased and was pleased to see those worry lines soften. "Come on. Nurse Carol's giving us the eye. We better get situated."

Picking up the mat, he followed Maria across the room to the spot she'd indicated earlier. Taking a cue from the other men present, he unrolled the mat onto the floor. Then he offered her his hand.

"Thanks," she murmured as she took his hand and lowered herself to the mat. She stretched out her legs in front of her.

Steven knelt beside her, but the images of the woman giving birth in the film continued to linger in his mind. He stared at Maria, noted the fit of the green slacks and the bright green, red and white maternity sweater she wore. She was small, nearly a foot shorter than his own six foot three inches. And despite the fact that she was nearly seven months pregnant, her arms and legs remained slim, almost willowy. Were it not for the bulge in her belly, no one would even know she was pregnant.

For the life of him, he couldn't imagine her small body going through the agony of giving birth.

"Steven, are you sure nothing's wrong?" Maria asked, tipping her head slightly to look up at him.

"I was…I was thinking about you having the baby." He paused and decided to come clean about his fears. "You're so small. What if the baby's too big? I was a big baby, nearly twelve pounds."

She patted his hand and gave him a look filled with humor and patience. "Well, I hope this baby isn't quite so big. But if it is and there's any sign of a problem during the delivery, the doctor will probably just do a C-section."

"A C-section? Oh God," he said on a groan. He felt the blood drain from his head at the thought of Maria being cut open to remove the baby.

"Don't look so worried. Women have been having babies for thousands of years. Our bodies know what to do."

"You saw that film. How can you sound so calm? Aren't you afraid?"

"A little," she told him. "But I'm excited, too."

"So was I—before I saw what you have to go through. Now I'm terrified," he admitted.

Maria laughed, a genuine laugh, among the few he'd heard from her since his arrival in Silver Valley. "It won't be that bad."

He arched his brow, letting her know he thought otherwise.

"Oh, all right. So it's not going to be a picnic. But feeling our baby growing inside me and knowing that soon I'll be able to hold him or her in my arms…well, it seems such a small price to pay for something so remarkable."

Our baby.

It had been the first time since she'd told him she was pregnant that she had actually referred to the child she was carrying as their child and not just hers. He clung to those words, took encouragement from them.

"All right, mothers and coaches. Take your positions," Nurse Carol ordered, cutting off further conversation.

Maria lay down flat on the mat and Steven waited beside her as the instructor took them through a series of steps that included the breaking of the water and the timing of the labor pains.

"Okay, the labor pains are now two minutes apart," Nurse Carol informed them. "What do you do?"

"Break out the cigars," one expectant father said, which resulted in a burst of laughter and an equal number of groans from the other ten couples.

"Not in my delivery room you don't—unless you're prepared to eat it," Nurse Carol remarked. Given the no-nonsense look in her eyes, Steven didn't think she was kidding.

"Mothers, what should your coaches do?"

"Buy us diamonds and flowers," a buxom redhead suggested.

"Naturally. But he should do that *after* the baby is born," Nurse Carol said. "Until then, what's his job?"

"To hold our hand and tell us to breathe," replied a tiny blonde who looked like she was carrying a watermelon.

"Very good, Penny. Coaches, take your partner's hand."

Kneeling beside Maria, Steven held her hand in his. And despite the well-lit room, the other couples and Nurse Carol barking out instructions, he felt an intimacy with Maria unlike any he'd ever known before. Something shifted inside him as he looked at her, her belly swollen with his child, her hand clasped in his.

"Remember, moms, when those pains hit, squeeze your coach's hand. And, coaches, tell her to breathe."

"You're beautiful," Steven whispered.

For a moment, Maria ceased making the quick, panting breaths. Her eyes met his, held.

"Time for another labor pain," Nurse Carol advised. "Remember as the pains get sharper, you squeeze on your coach's hand and try to remember to breathe."

Maria squeezed his hand, panted, and never once did her eyes leave his. And in that moment, he felt all the distance she'd put between them both emotionally and physically for the past several months begin to fade.

Somehow they managed to get through the rest of the class. And by the time he pulled the SUV onto the road leading to the Calderones', Steven knew that he and Maria had turned a corner. "It's pretty isolated out here," he noted as the solitary house came into view. "A lot different from Boston."

"Yes," Maria replied. "It's beautiful and peaceful, but I'm not sure I could ever live here the way Louis and Magdalene do. I guess I'm too used to having lots of family around. Even though Gina, Rita and I each had our own apartment in the brownstone, we were always in and out of each other's places. It was the same thing when Karen moved in."

"You miss them."

"Yes," Maria admitted as he pulled the SUV into the drive. He shoved the gear shaft into Park and cut off the engine. "It looks like we beat Magdalene and Louis home. I guess the meeting ran over."

"Why don't I come in and stay with you until they get back?" he offered.

"Thanks but I think I'll just turn in. I'm pretty tired." She unhooked her seat belt. "Thanks for coming with me tonight."

"I was happy to do it."

"Well, I'd better get inside before we both freeze sitting out here. Don't bother getting out. You should probably head back to the hotel before the snow starts again."

Steven didn't even bother responding. He simply exited the vehicle, went around to the passenger side and opened the door for her. "Thanks," she said as he helped her down to the driveway. Her boots moved silently across the fresh snow as she made her way to the front of the house.

Steven followed her, trying to use his body to shield her from the wind that had kicked up and whistled eerily through the pine trees. A solitary light had been left burning over the doorway. When she paused and turned to face him, her face was bathed in the soft light. Steven felt that tightening of emotion in his chest again as he looked at her. "Maria—"

"Steven—" she said at the same time.

He laughed. So did she. "You go first," he told her.

"I just wanted to say that I'm glad you came with me tonight."

"Me, too," he replied.

"And I'm sorry I didn't tell you about the baby sooner. You were right. This is your child, too."

She wet her lips as she spoke, and his gaze locked on the movement, reminding him of how long it had been since he'd kissed her, since she'd kissed him.

"And regardless of what happens between us, you are the baby's father. You should be a part of its life."

He captured her fingers, held them in his and moved in close. "I want to be a part of both your lives. Marry me." And before she could refuse him, he lowered his mouth to hers. He kissed her gently at first, soft, tender kisses, trying to show her how much he loved her, how much he wanted her. But when she opened to him, he groaned and took the kiss deeper. He kissed her hungrily, reveled in the feel of her arms wrapped around him, her fingers tangling in his hair.

When she tore her mouth free and clung to him, Steven held her close. All the while he continued to press kisses to her hair, drew in her scent. "I've missed you so much, Maria. I don't ever want to be away from you like this again."

"I've missed you, too," she admitted. "Let's go inside."

Holding her by the shoulders, he moved back a step so that he could see her face. Her cheeks were flushed, her eyes soft and dreamy, her lips swollen from their kisses. "If I go inside with you now, I'm not sure I'll be able to keep my hands off of you."

"I know. I don't want you to," she whispered.

Desire, already burning hot inside him, reached flash point. Everything told him to scoop Maria up into his arms, carry her inside to her bedroom and make love to her as they both wanted to do.

And if he did so now without first resolving things between them, he would be right back where they had been months ago—engaged in a secret affair and hiding their relationship from the world. He wanted more, deserved more. They both did. "If I come inside and I touch you, I do so as your future husband. No more sneaking around. No more hiding our relationship. We get married and go back to Boston together and tell our families everything.''

Maria pulled away from him. ''That's blackmail,'' she accused.

''Call it whatever you want. But that's the deal,'' he said, hoping he could make her understand that they deserved this chance. ''So what's it going to be? Do I come inside or do I go back to my hotel?''

''I guess you'd better go back to your hotel.''

Six

Something soft and fuzzy tickled Maria's cheek. She twitched her nose and snuggled her face back into the pillow. Moments later she felt the tickling sensation again and swiped the fur away.

Fur?

She opened her eyes and stared at the source of the fur. Sophia, Louis's pampered gray cat, lay curled up on the pillow next to Maria's head, her long fluffy tail swishing slightly while she enjoyed some feline dream. Normally, the cat followed Louis around the ranch like a dog, trailing behind him as he did his chores. Not even the snowfall seemed to deter Sophia from following her master. And when Louis was indoors, she was constantly on his lap.

"Sophia, what are you doing in here? Why aren't you with Louis?"

The cat opened her green eyes, stared directly at Maria. She gave Maria a look that seemed to say "It should be pretty obvious what I'm doing. I'm trying to sleep." Then she yawned, closed her eyes again and settled back down to sleep.

"Well, don't let me disturb you," Maria muttered. Pushing herself up on her elbows, she shoved the hair out of her eyes and checked the bedside clock. "Oh God," she groaned when she saw it was well past ten o'clock in the morning. She should have been up hours ago. Although she no longer needed to be at Baronessa Gelateria for the start of the day, she had continued to rise early. She never slept this late.

Not that she'd slept all that much, Maria admitted as she exited the bed and headed for the bathroom. She'd spent most of the night tossing and turning, thinking about Steven and wishing she knew what to do. Moments later, she stepped into the shower, and as the warm water washed over her body, she thought again of Steven. Of the way he had looked at her during the Lamaze class. Of how it had felt to have him there with her, sharing the experience. Of the way he had held and kissed her later. Of the things he'd said. If she hadn't already been in love with him, she'd have fallen in love with him last night. She'd offered him her body and he'd turned her down because he'd wanted more than sex from her. He'd wanted her heart. His honesty and integrity had shamed her. And his words about love and commitment, about taking chances, had kept her up most of the night.

Was Steven right? Would their families accept a marriage between them? Should she take a chance?

She thought about her conversation with her cousin, how Karen had said her parents were worried. Soapy water sluiced down her shoulders, her breasts, over her belly. Whether she married Steven or not, she would have to tell her parents and the rest of the family about the baby.

What about the Contis? How would they take the news?

Recalling Karen's remark, she imagined an angry Lucia confronting her father. Try as she might, she couldn't help but think of the Conti curse. And thoughts of the curse set off that flutter of panic inside her again. Exiting the shower, she grabbed a towel and after drying off, she began to dress.

Maria had just finished blow-drying her hair and pulling it back with a navy ribbon when the bathroom door creaked open.

"Meow."

"Still here?" she asked Sophia who began to wind herself around Maria's ankles. "Let's go see where Louis and Magdalene are."

Picking up the cat, she headed downstairs, fully expecting to smell the spicy scent of the enchiladas that Magdalene had promised to prepare for Louis's lunch that day. But when she reached the bottom of the staircase, she didn't smell enchiladas or anything else cooking for that matter. The house, usually abuzz with the sound of Magdalene's voice either singing along with the radio or more often than not during these past few weeks chatting on the phone about the upcoming Christmas Bazaar, was eerily silent.

"Magdalene?" she called out as uneasiness began to trip down her spine.

When no one answered, she put Sophia down and the cat scampered off in the direction of the kitchen. Maria followed—only to discover the room empty. No pots or pans simmered on the stove. She touched the oven, found it cold. A quick scan of the kitchen revealed no evidence that Magdalene had even been in the room that morning.

Something was wrong.

No sooner had the thought entered her head before Maria did her best to quell it. Since becoming pregnant, she'd developed a tendency to overreact. Magdalene probably just wasn't in the mood to cook today, she reasoned.

Leaving the kitchen, she checked first the den and then the room that had been set up as an office for Louis. Both were empty. She knocked on the couple's bedroom door. "Magdalene?" she called out before pushing the door open. The bed was made. The bag with Magdalene's knitting sat next to the chair. A book rested on a night table. But there was no sign of Magdalene.

Quickly Maria checked the remainder of the house, including the laundry room, but no signs of Magdalene. She thought about the garden. Since the first snowfall, the older woman hadn't spent much time there, but Maria decided to check it out anyway. Grabbing her coat, she headed outdoors.

A light snow was falling onto the already snow-covered ground as Maria made her way to the small garden out back. When she found it empty, she headed for the barn, burrowing into her coat and scarf as the wind whipped snow around her. Taking care, she planted her boots firmly along the path. Since Louis had moved most of his stock a few weeks ago, he'd taken to working in the barn and fussing over the four horses that he kept there. Magdalene was probably with him, she reasoned, thinking once again what a close relationship the couple shared.

When she reached the barn, she used both hands to

grip the handle on the heavy door and pulled it open. "Louis? Magdalene? Are you in here?" she called out as she stepped inside out of the cold. Adjusting her eyes to the dim light, she scanned the area to her left and then to her right. The smell of horses and hay was strong, but there was no sound of whinnying, no hooves pawing the floor. She moved over to the tack stall, found it empty. Also missing was the horse trailer.

Growing more anxious by the moment, Maria hurried back toward the house. She checked the garage and discovered Magdalene's Ford Explorer was there, but Louis's Range Rover was gone. Evidently the pair had gone off somewhere together. The realization should have calmed her. But it didn't. Probably because Magdalene made such a fuss about not leaving her alone in her pregnant condition, Maria thought. Telling herself she was being foolish, Maria had just exited the garage when she spied Louis's Range Rover turning onto the road. Despite the cold and wind, she waited for them, waving and smiling as they drove the big red vehicle up the driveway and entered the detached garage.

"I was beginning to worry about you," Maria called out when the garage door opened.

"We went to bring the horses to Arturo's," Magdalene informed her as she exited the garage.

Maria took one look at her friend's face and her smile faded. Something was wrong. The normally cheerful Magdalene looked as though she'd just lost her best friend. Louis looked even worse. "What's wrong?" she asked as they drew closer to the house. "Has something happened?"

"It is Louis's father. He's been in a car accident and is in the hospital in Billings," Magdalene explained.

Get FREE BOOKS and a FREE GIFT when you play the...

LAS VEGAS GAME

Just scratch off the gold box with a coin. Then check below to see the gifts you get!

YES! I have scratched off the gold Box. Please send me my **2 FREE BOOKS** and **gift for which I qualify.** I understand that I am under no obligation to purchase any books as explained on the back of this card.

326 SDL DUYF   225 SDL DUYV

FIRST NAME   LAST NAME

ADDRESS

APT.#   CITY

STATE/PROV.   ZIP/POSTAL CODE

(S D 03/03)

7	7	7

Worth TWO FREE BOOKS plus a BONUS Mystery Gift!

Worth TWO FREE BOOKS!

TRY AGAIN!

Visit us online at www.eHarlequin.com

Offer limited to one per household and not valid to current Silhouette Desire® subscribers. All orders subject to approval.

◄ DETACH AND MAIL CARD TODAY! ▼

BUSINESS REPLY MAIL
FIRST-CLASS MAIL   PERMIT NO. 717-003   BUFFALO, NY

POSTAGE WILL BE PAID BY ADDRESSEE

SILHOUETTE READER SERVICE
3010 WALDEN AVE
PO BOX 1867
BUFFALO NY 14240-9952

NO POSTAGE
NECESSARY
IF MAILED
IN THE
UNITED STATES

"I'm so sorry," Maria told them. "Is he... Will he be all right?"

"We don't know yet. He is in a coma," Louis said, his voice holding the same stricken note as his face. He opened the door for them to enter the house.

"Papa Calderone is a strong man," Magdalene told her husband as they removed their coats and hung them on the rack near the door. She touched her husband's arm. "He will get through this, Louis."

Louis covered the hand that rested on his arm. "I hope you are right."

"I am," Magdalene insisted and Maria was sure the other woman was trying to be strong for her husband.

"If I hope to reach Billings before dark, I better go pack."

"I'll fix some snacks for the drive."

"You don't need to do that. I will pick up something."

"I *said* I will fix you something," Magdalene insisted.

Louis sighed. "All right. But do not make a fuss. I am really not hungry."

Magdalene stood and watched as her husband headed in the direction of the bedroom. "My poor Louis. He has not eaten a bite since his sister called this morning to tell us Papa Calderone was in the hospital. And you know how he loves to eat."

"I'm sure he's just worried," Maria offered, wanting to ease her friend's anxiety. "How are you holding up?"

"All right, I guess." Magdalene swiped at her eyes. "I'd better go fix those sandwiches," she said and together they headed for the kitchen.

While Magdalene pulled out assorted meats and cheeses, Maria got out the home-baked bread that Magdalene preferred to the store-bought variety and began to slice it. "Do they know what happened?" Maria asked.

"According to Louis's sister Anna, a drunk driver apparently crossed the highway median and collided with Papa Calderone's truck."

"How awful."

Magdalene nodded. She slathered mayonnaise and mustard onto the bread. "The other car hit Papa's truck head-on. The doctors think his head must have hit the windshield. He has a bad concussion and broke his collarbone and arm. Anna says Papa lost consciousness on the way to the hospital and has been in the coma ever since."

Maria went to her friend, took the sandwiches from her, set them aside and hugged her. "Magdalene, I am so sorry."

"Thank you." Magdalene sniffed and stepped back. She retrieved the sandwich wrap. "The doctors say the longer he's in the coma, the worse his chances of recovering are."

Maria took the cellophane from Magdalene. "I'll do this. Why don't you brew a pot of coffee." As Magdalene busied herself with making coffee, Maria proceeded to wrap up the sandwiches. "Head injuries can be tricky. I don't think even the doctors understand them fully. The good thing is that he's in the hospital and getting good care."

Magdalene finished measuring the coffee grounds and switched on the coffeepot, then she picked up a dish towel to wipe her hands. "How could something like this happen?" she asked, her voice breaking, her fingers curling into the dishcloth. "And why now when it's so close to Christmas? If Papa Calderone does not make it, it will kill my Louis."

Maria stuffed the sandwiches into the padded food carrier and went to her friend. "You mustn't think like that. I've read about people who are in a coma for months, even years, and then one day they just wake up and are fine. You and Louis just need to hang in there."

"You're right," Magdalene said and wiped the tears from her cheeks. "I am sorry."

"There's nothing to be sorry about. Now why don't you let me finish this up while you go pack so that you and Louis can get on the road."

"But I am not going with Louis," Magdalene informed her.

"Why ever not?"

"Because we do not know how long Louis will need to stay in Billings. It may only be for a few days. But it could be longer."

"But I thought… Isn't that why you took the horses to Arturo's?"

Magdalene shook her head. "Louis did not want me to have to worry about caring for them in case…in case he needs to stay."

"But I still don't understand why you aren't going with him. If it's because you're worried about Sophia, I can take care of her for you."

"Maria, it is not Sophia that I am concerned about leaving. It is you."

Maria blinked. "Me? But why?"

"Because, *ma pequeña,* you're in the last trimester of your pregnancy. What if your baby should decide to come early?"

"The baby's not due for another two months," Maria pointed out.

"True. But sometimes a baby decides to come early. Louis's sister Anna's first child was six weeks early."

"Honestly, Magdalene—"

"And what if, Heaven forbid," she began while making the sign of the cross, "you should trip or have an accident? Who would be here to take care of you?"

"I'm not going to have an accident," Maria insisted. "And you have my promise that I'll be extra careful. Now please, go pack your things and go with Louis."

"I cannot leave you here alone."

At a loss as to what to do to convince her friend, Maria suggested, "Do you want me to come with you and Louis?"

"Oh no. The long drive would be hard on you and the baby."

"I suppose I could go home," Maria said, even though just the idea of returning to Boston now and facing everyone had her stomach knotting.

"No, *pequeña*. I do not want you to leave until you are ready. And somehow, I think you are not ready. I am right. Yes?"

"Yes," Maria admitted. "But Louis needs you. So does your family. And I know you want to go with him."

Magdalene patted her hand. "Were I to go, I would be worried about you here all alone. No. It is impossible. Louis will go and I will stay."

"Magdalene, please. Isn't there anything I can do or say to convince you to go?"

"Well, there is one thing," she said, a gleam coming into her eyes.

"What?"

"If you were to have someone…say, Steven staying here with you, then I would feel better about leaving because I would know you would not be alone."

"Impossible."

"Why? He loves you and he is your baby's father. Who better to protect you than him?"

"No. It's a bad idea." Just the thought of staying alone in the house with Steven had her heart racing like a freight train.

"Then I will stay here with you and Louis will go to Billings alone. Now I had better go see if he needs any help packing," she said and started to leave the room.

"Magdalene, wait!"

Magdalene paused, looked back at her.

Maria couldn't help feeling as though she were trapped between a rock and a hard place. But she hated to be the reason that Magdalene stayed behind when it was so obvious that Louis and her family needed her. "What if…what if I agreed to have Steven check in on me and promised to call him if I should have any problems? Would you go with Louis to Billings then?"

"You would speak with him every day and promise to call him if you needed his help?"

"Yes. I promise."

"Very well. Then I will go with my Louis."

"And Louis's father is doing all right?" Maria asked Magdalene as they spoke on the phone three days later.

"He is out of the coma and it will take some time for his injuries to heal, but the doctors say he may be able to go home day after tomorrow."

"I'm so glad for you both," Maria told her friend.

"And how are you? Has Steven been checking in on you?" Magdalene asked, the questions racing out one behind the other.

"I'm fine, Magdalene. And yes, Steven has been over here twice and called at least a dozen times to make sure that I'm okay." And each time she was with him, spoke to him, she was finding it more and more difficult not to do as he asked and marry him. If only their families didn't hate each other and things hadn't become even worse because of this mess with her cousin Derrick.

"Maria, are you still there?"

"Sorry," Maria replied, dragging her thoughts back to the conversation.

"Louis wants to know how Sophia is."

Maria grinned. "Sophia's fine. She misses you, but I'm doing my best to keep her company," she said and stroked the pampered cat who'd perched on the night-stand in her demand for Maria's attention.

"It's supposed to be the other way around. She's sup-posed to keep you company."

"Try telling her that."

Magdalene laughed. "No doubt you are spoiling her more than Louis does."

"That would be difficult," Maria teased, since she knew that Louis catered to the silver-colored feline who managed to weave her body between the phone's cord and the cradle.

"You are sure if we stay in Billings a few more days that you will be okay by yourself?"

"I'm sure," Maria promised and after swearing to call Steven if anything should happen, Maria ended the call. She finished dressing and set about tidying up her room. When she finished, the house seemed suddenly huge and lonely. She thought about her parents' home, of how it had always been so busy and filled with people when she'd been growing up. Even when she'd moved out and into the townhouse with her sisters, she'd seldom been alone. Suddenly lonely and growing more than a little homesick, she debated whether to call her parents again.

And what would you tell them, Maria? That you're pregnant and the father of your child is a Conti?

No, her folks deserved to hear that news from her in person, not on the telephone with so many miles separating them. Maybe if she spoke with Karen, she'd be able to shake this melancholy, Maria decided

"Hi this is Karen," the answering machine picked up after the fourth ring. "Ash and I aren't available at the moment, but if you'll leave a message at the sound of the tone, we'll get back to you as soon as we can."

Maria left a message and after ending the call, she considered calling Steven. And tell him what? She still didn't know what she was going to do and she wasn't sure his plan of action—getting married—was the right answer. So she hung up the phone. Determined to shake off her ennui, Maria said, "Come on, Sophia. Why don't we surprise Magdalene and Louis by baking them some special treats for when they get home?"

Then she headed out of the bedroom, unaware that as Sophia leapt from the nightstand to follow her, she knocked the telephone receiver from its cradle.

"With this much snow on the road and at the speed you were going, you're lucky you didn't wrap this fancy piece of machinery around a tree," the state trooper told Steven while he wrote out a speeding citation. Apparently the big burly guy was used to the frigid blasts of wind because he continued to fill out the ticket with painstaking slowness. "I don't know how the folks in Boston feel about speeding, but here in Montana, we expect folks to honor the speed limits posted."

"I understand," Steven replied, anxious to get this over with so he could get to the Calderones' place and check on Maria. After being unable to reach her all morning on her cell phone and getting a continuous busy signal on the Calderones' phone line, he'd convinced the operator to break in on the line at the Calderone Ranch and check for conversation. Sure enough, there had been no one on the line. Which meant the phone, for some reason, was off the hook. Of course, imagining why had sent fear firing through him like a bullet.

What if Maria had had an accident? What if one of those huge pines had fallen onto the house and trapped her inside? What if something had happened to her and even now she was lying on the floor unconscious and hurt?

The trooper handed him the pad and pen. "I'll need your signature."

Steven scrawled his name across the bottom of the slip with fingers that felt like ice since he'd taken off his gloves when he'd produced his driver's license. He handed the pad and pen back to the other man.

The trooper tore the citation off the pad and handed it to him. "Instructions are on the back about paying the fine. Of course, you can make a court appearance if you want to contest it."

"I don't," Steven told him and tucked the ticket in the Explorer's console. "That is, I don't want to contest the ticket. I'll mail in the fine."

The trooper nodded, sending a layer of snow falling from the brim of his hat. "Just make sure you keep it slow the rest of the way."

"I will," Steven assured him, itching to get on his way.

The trooper tucked his pad of tickets into his back pocket, but made no attempt to move away from the Explorer. "You might also want to stay put when you reach wherever it is you're in such a hurry to get to because if this snow keeps up, the roads are going to get a lot worse.''

''I'm on my way to pick up my fiancé and take her back into town.'' Or at least he was going to try to convince Maria to come with him.

''I wouldn't count on making it back tonight. If we get as much snow as the weather guys are predicting, I expect the roads are gonna be shut down. You'd do better to just stay at her place.''

''Thanks. I'll do that.'' And whether Maria liked it or not, he was spending the night because he had no intention of leaving her alone again—not with this monster snowstorm brewing.

Once the trooper stepped away from his vehicle, Steven started his engine and got back onto the road. Though it cost him, he forced himself to drive more slowly. Finally, what seemed to be an eternity later, he pulled his Explorer into the Calderones' drive. He'd barely shut off the engine before he was racing across the snow-covered ground to the front door.

He punched the doorbell. One. Two. Three. Four. Five seconds ticked by during which the wind howled like a banshee as it swept through the tall pines. Snow continued to fall and blanket the already white landscape. And the sky that had been filled with clouds that were heavy with snow at daybreak had turned an ugly shade of gray.

Impatient, Steven leaned on the buzzer again. When no one answered, the acid that had begun to churn in his stomach when he'd been told there was a problem with the Calderone phone line burned even hotter. He tried the door, found it locked. ''Damn,'' he hissed, remembering he was the one who had insisted yesterday that Maria keep the door locked since she was alone.

''Maria!'' He pounded on the door with his fist and

tried the doorknob again. He swore, then tried pounding harder. And when he got no response, he trounced through the snow to a window and attempted to see if he could detect any movement behind the drapes. But he couldn't see a thing and thanks to the wind, he couldn't hear anything either.

With panic racing through his veins, he headed around to the back of the house. Snow pummelled his face and body like bullets as he made his way to the rear of the ranch-style house, hoping to find the kitchen door unlocked. When he turned the corner and saw the light blazing from the kitchen window, he ran until he reached the door. This time he didn't bother knocking; he simply yanked on the doorknob. And he swore when he found it locked.

"Maria," he yelled again and pounded on the door with both fists. Frustrated, he stepped back and then slammed his shoulder into the door. The door didn't give, but he immediately saw stars from the impact. He was about to head out to the barn in search of a crowbar or some other tool with which to break in when the door suddenly opened.

"Steven," Maria said his name in a breathless rush.

Steven froze for a second as relief washed through him. He didn't think. He simply reacted. Grabbing her by the shoulders, he dragged her against him, not caring that he was cold and his jacket was covered in snow. "Are you all right?" he demanded, all the while rubbing his hands down her back and holding her tighter. He pressed his face into her hair, not caring that they were standing just outside the door and that snow was falling on them both.

"I'm fine," she said in a muffled voice against his chest.

"Thank God," he murmured as he continued to hold her, touch her, breathe in her scent. Not until a shiver went through her and into him did Steven register that she was standing outside in a blizzard without a coat. "Come on," he all but growled the words and hauled her into the house with him. Then he slammed the door closed.

"Steven—"

"Give me a minute," he commanded. Despite his relief, fear-induced adrenaline still pumped through his veins. Trying to get a grip on the emotions storming inside him, he kept his back to her while he tore off his snow-covered jacket and tossed it on a chair, heedless of the clumps of snow that fell to the floor.

"You're making a mess on Magdalene's floor," she accused and started to retrieve his jacket.

"Leave it."

"I'll do no such thing," she informed him.

Lightning quick, he caught her by the shoulders and hauled her up against him again. "I don't know whether to strangle you or kiss you."

She blinked. Then temper flared in her brown eyes. An angry flush colored her cheeks. "You'll do neither."

"Wrong," he said just before his mouth crashed down on hers. He kissed her hard. He kissed her fast. He kissed her with all the fear that had been knotted in his gut like a fist because he'd been unable to reach her. Anchoring her head in his hands, he demanded a response.

Maria gave it to him, winding her arms around his neck and opening her mouth to him. He ravaged her mouth with his tongue, with his teeth, with his lips. She responded by nipping his lower lip, by dueling with her tongue. When she gasped, he drank in the sound and taste of her. Still, it wasn't enough. So he kissed her again and again and again. He was no longer sure where her mouth began and his ended.

Steven didn't know how long he stood there feeding on her mouth. It could have been a minute. It could have been an hour. Not until Maria caught his face in her hands and eased away did any semblance of time come back to him.

"You want to tell me what that was all about?" she asked, her voice soft, her eyes warm.

"I—" Steven took in her swollen mouth, the marks on her face from his whisker-rough skin. Appalled by his actions, he rubbed a hand down his face. Then he remembered the hours of trying to reach her without success and that knot of fear in his gut during the drive out there. "I thought something had happened to you. That you were hurt, maybe even unconscious."

"Why on earth would you think that?"

"Because I've been trying to reach you on the phone for hours and couldn't get through."

"But I haven't been on the phone," she argued.

"So I discovered when I finally convinced the operator that it was an emergency and that she had to break in on the line and check for conversation. The phone's off the hook."

As if she doubted him, Maria walked over to the wall phone in the kitchen and picked up the receiver. They both could hear the beeping that indicated a problem on the phone line. She flushed and hung up the phone. "I guess one of the phones must have been knocked off the hook," she offered. "You should have tried my cell phone."

"I did," he informed her. "You didn't answer. Nor did you respond to any of the messages I left you."

"You must have dialed the wrong number."

"I didn't. If you don't believe me, check your cell phone."

"Fine," she said and marched over to the table and snatched up her purse. She began pawing through its contents. After a moment, she said, "I must have left it in my car," her flush deepening. "That doesn't give you the right to show up here acting all macho."

"No?" he countered, his voice hard. Now that he knew she was okay, the panic was gone. So was the fear. In their place was a new kind of tension born from that steamy kiss. He registered the Christmas music playing, knew instinctively that she had no idea about the dangerous weather conditions. "When's the last time you turned on the television or the radio and listened to a weather report? Better yet, when's the last time you even bothered to look outside?"

"I...I've been busy."

He glanced over at the countertops, noted the iced cookies and treats. "Too busy apparently to realize that you're out here in the middle of nowhere all alone and pregnant and that there's a damn blizzard going on outside."

"A blizzard?"

"Yes, Maria, a blizzard." He caught her by the arm, marched her over to the door and threw it open. "Take a look," he commanded, gesturing toward the white landscape where the snow drifts were quickly approaching three feet.

"Oh," she whispered.

When she shivered, he slammed the door closed. "And according to the state trooper who stopped me on my way here for speeding, it's going to get a hell of a lot worse."

She pulled free of his grasp and stepped away. She

crossed her arms over her chest and tipped up her chin defiantly. "Then you'd better go. Otherwise, you're liable to have trouble getting back to town."

"I'm not going anywhere."

"But—"

"It's not up for discussion," he told her. "That's my baby you're carrying and there's no way I'm leaving you alone out here."

"Then I'll go back with you to the city and get a room at the hotel."

"Forget it. We're better off staying here until this storm's over."

"I don't want to stay here with you," she argued.

The rejection stung—more than it should, Steven thought. "That's too bad because you don't have any choice."

"I—"

"Dammit, Maria! The roads are closed."

Seven

Maria desperately wanted to argue with Steven, but she knew that he was right. She had been foolish not to pay closer attention to the weather. But she'd awakened feeling lonely and homesick and confused, so she'd thrown herself into baking some holiday treats for the Calderones and her family. "I guess I really don't have any choice, do I?"

"No."

She sighed and couldn't help feeling a flicker of annoyance when Sophia waltzed into the kitchen and immediately trotted over to Steven. "Then I'd better see that the extra bedroom has clean sheets and towels."

"While you do that I'll check the phone extensions and see which one's off the hook."

"I'll do it," Maria told him. She already suspected it was the one in her bedroom.

"Fine." He walked over to the chair to retrieve his

jacket and Sophia followed him, weaving herself in and
out of his legs as he shrugged into the coat.

"Where are you going?"

"To take a look at the generator. Louis showed me
where it is and I want to make sure I'm familiar with it
in case the power goes out."

"Traitor," she muttered when Sophia darted out of
the door and followed Steven. Feeling annoyed with herself, Steven and the cat, Maria headed upstairs. Much to
her chagrin, she spied the phone dislodged from the cradle on her nightstand, beeping in distress. Striding across
the room, she righted the receiver, then she headed down
the hall to the spare bedroom. She put fresh sheets on
the bed and made sure there were extra towels in the
bathroom that adjoined the two rooms before heading
back downstairs.

She'd just returned to the kitchen when the door
opened. Sophia raced inside, her gray fur dusted in
white, and Steven, who stomped his boots and managed
to shake off some of the snow, came in behind her, his
arms loaded with firewood.

"Could you get the door for me?" he asked.

Maria rushed over and closed the door behind him,
shutting out the gust of cold air that whipped through
the room. She followed Steven to the den where he began filling the bin next to the fireplace with wood.

"I checked out the generator and it looks like it's
ready to go if we need it," he said as he stacked the
wood. "But I figured it would be a good idea to bring
in some extra wood just in case."

"You're probably right," she said and realized she
should have thought of that herself. While Steven
worked, Maria went to the hall to retrieve her coat and
scarf. Pulling on her gloves, she returned to the den.

"Where do you think you're going?" Steven asked as he stood.

"To help you carry in some more wood."

"I can handle it. You stay in here where it's warm."

Steven's dismissal did nothing to improve her mood. "Don't treat me like a simpering, helpless female, Steven," she countered. "A little snow isn't going to hurt me and I'm certainly capable of carrying in firewood."

Steven let out a breath. "Trust me, no one could ever accuse you of being simpering or helpless. I have no doubt you can handle anything that's thrown at you. But you just happen to be seven months pregnant and there's a blizzard going on out there and we're stranded here for Lord knows how long. Why chance catching your death of cold or tripping or doing anything that might put you and the baby at risk unless you have to?"

His reply deflated all her righteous indignation in one fell swoop. Of course, he was right. Only an idiot would think otherwise. And though she felt like an idiot at the moment, she hadn't completely taken leave of her senses. "I'm sorry. I just feel...useless."

Steven walked over to her, pressed a kiss to her forehead. "Never," he said with a smile. "I'll be back in a minute and maybe when I finish I can convince you to let me sample some of those goodies I saw in the kitchen."

She not only allowed him to sample the goodies in the kitchen, she served him a plate filled with the assorted cookies, candies and cakes. She refilled the coffee cup in front of him and poured herself a cup of the hot chocolate she'd prepared.

"What do you call these shell-shaped things?" Steven

asked as he picked up the chocolate cookie dusted with powdered sugar and devoured it.

"Those are Madeleines."

"They're fabulous." He reached for another cookie. "And this?"

"Swiss-Italian chocolate meringues."

He closed his eyes and moaned. "These are sinful."

Maria laughed. "That's what my grandfather used to say. It's my grandmother Angelica's recipe."

"I didn't realize your grandmother was a baker. I'd always heard that the gelato was her passion."

"It was," Maria replied. "But she was very good at a lot of things." Much better than she was, Maria thought silently.

"So is her granddaughter."

"Thanks." Feeling restless, she brought her cup to the sink, filled it with water. "Do you want more coffee?"

"No thanks." He pushed away from the table and brought his empty cup and plate over to her at the sink. "That was great. Thanks."

"You're welcome," she said and rinsed out the china pieces before putting them into the dishwasher. After drying off her hands, she walked over to the cabinet and began removing containers for the baked goods.

"Here, let me get that for you," Steven offered as he came up behind her and retrieved the plastic containers from the top shelf.

"Thanks," she murmured and returned to the counter where she began placing the Madeleines inside one of the bins.

"Need some help?"

"No. I can manage."

He ignored her and taking one of the other plastic

containers, he began placing the meringue cookies inside. "All of this for the church bazaar?"

"No. It's for the Calderones and my family," Maria told him. "These are some of my family's favorites. My grandmother always spent the first two weeks in December baking up a storm before the caroling party and I used to help her."

"The caroling party?"

"It's tradition for all the Barones to go Christmas caroling the week before Christmas," Maria explained, smiling at the memory. "We're not very good and I suspect a lot of the neighbors wish we wouldn't. But we brave the cold anyway and try to make some semblance of carrying a tune so that we can go home and reward ourselves for our efforts by stuffing ourselves with cookies and chocolate."

"It sounds like a nice tradition."

"It is." And just thinking about it made her homesick all over again. "What about you? Does your family have any silly holiday traditions they observe?"

"My aunt Lucia always serves her famous eggnog on Christmas Eve."

"That's nice."

"No, it's not. The stuff is awful."

"Steven," Maria admonished, even though her lips twitched in amusement. "What a terrible thing to say."

"It's the truth. Aunt Lucia's eggnog could put hair on a person's chest and probably did put the hair on mine," he said, humor and affection in his voice.

"Then why drink it?"

"Because she thinks we love the stuff. And no one has the heart to tell her how bad it really is." He shrugged. "Besides, she only makes it once a year."

Moved by his sensitivity, she said, "You're a good man, Steven Conti."

"That's what I keep telling you," he said as he swiped one of the Madeleines from the container she was filling and popped it into his mouth. "And everyone knows we good-guy types are hard to come by."

"Is that so?"

"Sure is."

She retrieved the lid to the container, prepared to seal it when Steven reached for another cookie. She swatted at his fingers, but not before allowing him his bounty.

He polished off the chocolate shell and grinned at her. "And being the smart woman that you are, you wouldn't want to let me get away, would you?"

"Wouldn't I?" she asked, surprising herself that she could tease with him so easily. Probably had something to do with the isolation, she reasoned. Right now Boston and their family problems seemed light-years away.

"Nope, you wouldn't. And sooner or later you're going to realize that and agree to marry me."

Deciding it best not to go down that road, Maria changed the subject. "Would you hand me that tray of pecan tassies on the end of the counter?"

"These little tarts with the gooey filling?" he asked, indicating the miniature tarts loaded with the pecan pie filling.

"Yes."

He handed the tray to her. "What did you call them?"

"Pecan tassies," she responded and began transferring the treats into another container.

"I don't think I got one of those."

"Here," Maria said and handed him one. Though she said nothing, she couldn't help but delight at his moans of pleasure.

"You going to send *all* of this to your family?" he asked.

"No," she said. "I packed away some for Louis and Magdalene. The rest I was planning to ship to my family with some Christmas gifts later this week."

"Don't you plan to go home for Christmas?"

"I haven't made up my mind yet," she told him. And it was true. She'd put off the decision for weeks now, unsure of how to tell her family about the baby, not wanting to see their shock and disappointment when she told them that Steven was the baby's father.

"You won't be able to keep the baby a secret much longer," Steven reminded her. "I'd like to be with you when you do tell them."

Maria gripped the countertop with both hands. Knowing how awful things had been between their families since the fire, she could only imagine how furious her parents and siblings would be. But it wasn't for herself that she feared. It was for Steven. "Please, can we talk about something else."

"All right," he said, and although he didn't pursue the topic, it was clear that he had wanted to.

"Have you finished your Christmas shopping yet?" she asked, determined to restore the easier mood.

"I haven't even started."

"You're kidding. What are you waiting for? Christmas is less than two weeks away."

"I still have plenty of time," he boasted and launched into how easy shopping actually was and how anyone who was organized could knock it out in a few hours.

And for the next thirty minutes, he amused Maria with tales of weird gifts received over the years and his approach to gifts for those hard-to-buy-for relatives and friends. By the time she sealed the last container of baked goods, she was laughing out loud. "You're making that up," she told him after one particularly outrageous claim of receiving chocolate-covered ants from a client.

"Scout's honor," he said, flashing her another smile that had the dimple winking in his cheek.

She gave him a dubious look before stacking the last container of baked goods with the others. "That's the last of it," she said. After wiping off her hands, she walked over to the window, pulled back the curtain and looked outside. To her surprise, darkness had set in. The snow continued to fall, more heavily now, weighing down the branches of the Ponderosa pines. In the far distance, she could make out the shadow of the mountains that stood like silent sentinels.

"You have to admit," Steven said, coming up behind her, "all that snow and the mountains make for a pretty sight."

"Yes," she replied. And a lonely one, too, she added in silence. Or perhaps it was she who was lonely, Maria thought. She pressed a hand to her lower back to ease the ache no doubt caused by being on her feet so long. "I'd better see about cleaning up those cookie sheets," she said and waited for Steven to step back. When he did, she walked over to the counter and began stacking the cookie sheets.

Steven held out his hands for the trays. When she hesitated, he said, "Why don't you let me wash these while you go stretch out on the couch for a while and rest?"

"But—"

"No 'buts,' Maria. Your back's hurting."

"How—"

"That's the third time in the past hour that you've rubbed it."

"You're very observant."

He touched her cheek. "Only where you're concerned."

She caught his hand. "Steven—"

"Humor me, Maria. You're carrying my baby and in a couple of months, you're going to give me the most wonderful gift a man could ever ask for—a child. The least I can do is wash up a few pans for you. Admit it, you're tired."

"Just a little," she conceded.

"Come on, then," he said and steered her out of the kitchen toward the den. "It's a little chilly in here. I'll get a fire going for you."

"You don't have to do that," she protested.

"I *want* to do it," he informed her. He motioned to the couches. "Go ahead and put your feet up and get comfortable while I see to the fire."

The idea of stretching out on the couch was too appealing to argue further. So she kicked off her shoes and curled up on the sofa, tucking her feet beneath her. She pulled the brightly colored afghan around her to ward off the chill. Sophia, who lay snuggled up across from her on Louis's chair, opened her eyes as though to check out the source of the intrusion. Just as quickly she closed them again.

Within moments flames leaped to life in the fireplace grate. Steven stood and dusted off his hands. "It should be all nice and toasty in here in a couple of minutes."

Maria stared at him, noted the lock of black hair that had fallen across his forehead, the way the firelight illuminated the sharpness of his cheekbones, the warmth and concern in his blue eyes. He looked so tall and handsome and strong standing there, she thought. Her heart swelled with love for him. "Thank you," she murmured.

"My pleasure. Now try to get some rest," he said. "I'll take care of the kitchen and be back in a few minutes."

It took him just over thirty minutes to set the kitchen to rights. A check of the weather gave no indication of the snow letting up. Not wanting to disturb Maria, he had put on the radio in the spare bedroom to get confirmation that they were indeed expecting blizzard conditions. The threat of the storm and the potential for them being stranded should have alarmed him, Steven thought. Instead he'd welcomed the isolation and the chance to be with Maria. Which just went to show how desperate he was to change her mind about marrying him, he admitted. Somehow, someway, he had to convince her and he had to do it soon. Because based on his last conversation with Ethan Mallory, the search for his sister was moving much too slowly. Thoughts of his sister being kidnapped by Derrick Barone had anger balling like a fist in his gut. He'd had enough of the bureaucracy. Bianca must be out of her mind with fear. If Mallory and the feds couldn't find Barone and get his sister back, then he damn well would.

Suddenly thoughts about his and Maria's families and their reactions to the situation settled over him like a dark cloud. He couldn't think about them now, Steven told himself. Right now he had to concentrate on Maria and try to convince her that they deserved a chance— not just for their sakes, but for the sake of their baby. With that thought and only that thought in his mind, he started for the den.

Only he found Maria sound asleep. And as he stared

at her, the spiel that he'd been practicing while he'd cleaned the kitchen was forgotten. Resting on her side, she had one hand tucked beneath her cheek. Her lips were slightly parted. Her hair framed her face like mocha silk and fanned out over the russet-colored pillow. Her skin looked like fine porcelain—smooth and perfect. There was something almost spiritual about the site of Maria in slumber, Steven thought as he moved closer. Standing over her, he took in her small body stretched out on the couch, the roundness of her stomach, the softness of her expression. God, but she was beautiful. Like a priceless work of art. Raphael's Madonna in the flesh, he decided. And for the first time in his life Steven wished he'd been blessed with the skill of an artist instead of a head for computers so that he could capture her on canvas.

He shifted his gaze to her belly, swollen with his child, and his throat tightened. He loved her, had loved her almost from the moment he'd first met her. Emotion swirled inside him so fiercely, it made his chest ache. He loved Maria and he'd be damned if he'd give up on them because of their families. Suddenly all the frustration that had been eating at him because of Maria's refusal to marry him reared its head again. He *would* have a life with Maria, he promised himself. Somehow he would convince her to give them a chance.

And what if Maria's right? What if in choosing her, you lose your family?

Then he would lose his family, Steven told himself. Because for him there could be only one choice—Maria. She was his past. She was his present. And without her, he had no future. Picking up the afghan from the floor where she had kicked it off, Steven draped the throw over her. Unable to resist, he leaned down and pressed a kiss to her lips.

Maria's lashes fluttered. She opened her eyes, stared up at him out of brown eyes soft and dreamy with sleep. "Steven?"

"Yes," he whispered. "I didn't mean to wake you. Go back to sleep."

"You're real, then? Not a dream?"

He smiled, smoothed the hair away from her brow. "I'm real."

She reached up, touched his face as though to assure herself he was indeed flesh and blood. "I was dreaming about you…about us."

He turned his face into her palm, kissed it. "I hope it was a good dream."

"It was," she said, a smile curving her lips. "We were at Nicholas and Gail's wedding. Only it wasn't their wedding, it was ours."

"I like the sound of your dream."

"But it was only a dream," she said, the smile fading. "It wasn't real."

"It can be real. I want it to be real," he told her. "I love you."

"And I love you. Oh—" she gasped.

"What is it?" he asked, the blood in his veins chilling as she clutched her stomach and took several sharp breaths. "What's wrong?"

She whooshed out another breath, then pushed up on her elbows so that she was half-sitting, half-reclining. "It's the baby. Our son or daughter decided to practice field goal kicks again."

"Field goal…" He shifted his gaze from her face to her belly and back again. To his surprise, she was grinning. "I don't understand. Are you all right? Is something wrong with the baby?"

"We're both fine."

"But you cried out… You were in pain," he argued.

"Just for a minute. Our baby packs quite a kick."

"Is that normal?" he asked, immediately concerned. He'd never spent any time around babies, or pregnant women for that matter. What he knew about both wouldn't fill a thimble.

"It's normal at this stage in the pregnancy."

Steven swallowed as he digested that information, awed by the evidence of the tiny life that they had created—a life that was now growing inside Maria. "Does it hurt very much?"

"Only for a second or two. It's more uncomfortable than anything. And surprising," she added while she smoothed a hand over her stomach. "I think our baby's impatient to be born."

"You're not…" He swallowed back the panic that was climbing in his throat and tried again. "You're not about to go into labor or anything, are you?"

Maria laughed. "No," she assured him and laughed even harder. "At least I hope not anytime soon."

Especially not when the nearest doctor was miles and miles away, he thought, worry settling over him again.

"Relax, Steven. The baby isn't due for another two months."

"But you said yourself, he or she is impatient to be born. What if—"

"Steven, the baby's just active. It doesn't mean I'm ready to have it. It just means— Oh, there it goes again," she said and grabbed his hand. She pressed it to her belly. "Can you feel it?"

Suddenly the baby kicked. Steven started. "I felt it,"

he said, awed by the sensation. When it kicked again, he broke out into a grin. "There it is again. Did you feel it?"

"Yes, I felt it," she said and gave him an indulgent smile.

"Dumb question, huh?" he countered, laughing at his own foolishness. "Of course, you felt it." But he couldn't help it, he had felt his son or daughter moving in Maria's womb for the first time.

"It is pretty amazing, isn't it?"

"*You're* the one who's amazing."

Her smile slipped a notch. "Not all that amazing. Neither one of us were planning on a baby and I got pregnant."

"I was there, remember?" He tipped up her chin, forced her to look at him. "We may not have planned it, but I'm happy about the baby, Maria. Are you?"

"Yes. I want this baby. I really do. I just wish…I just wish things could have been different."

"What? That it's father wasn't a Conti?" he asked, the accusation out before he could stop himself. Irritated with himself for lashing out as he had, he looked away. "I'm sorry," he muttered.

Maria touched his shoulder. "Look at me, Steven."

He turned toward her, prepared to see the rejection in her eyes. Instead there was only tenderness. "I'm glad you're my baby's father. When I said I wished things could be different, I meant the problems between our families."

"They're not our problems," he told her, relief flooding through him. Relief and hope. He caught her hands, held them in his and stared into her eyes. "The feud between our families has nothing to do with us. We won't let it."

"But it does and it will," she insisted.

"Maria—"

"I'm afraid, Steven. I'm afraid of the Conti curse. Of what might happen to our baby."

"I won't let anything happen to you or our baby," he promised. "What can I do to make you believe me?"

"I believe you'd do everything possible to protect us, but there are some things that not even you can control."

"Maria," he began, frustrated that he couldn't make her see that the curse was nothing more than a foolish superstition.

She pressed a finger to his lips. "Let's not argue."

"All right," he murmured against her fingertips.

When she struggled to get up, Steven took her hand and helped her to her feet. "Thanks," she said. "The bigger I get, the harder it is getting up and down. I probably look like a beached whale."

"I think you look beautiful."

"You're either being kind or you need glasses."

"I'm being honest. I don't think I've ever seen anyone more beautiful than you are at this moment."

She flushed. "Thank you."

"I'm the one who's grateful," he told her. And he was. Grateful that he'd found Maria and that she was going to have his child.

"Let's see if you're still grateful after I fix us dinner. My culinary talents are limited to cookies and gelato."

"Then why don't I make dinner?"

"You can cook?" Maria asked, a combination of surprise and skepticism in her tone.

Steven scoffed. "My family owns one of the best Italian restaurants in Boston. Of course I can cook. Any special requests?"

"Surprise me."

Eight

Steven surprised her by serving a superb chicken marinara with penne pasta, a green salad and some of Magdalene's homemade bread that he'd taken from the freezer, warmed and slathered with garlic butter. Suddenly it dawned on her that in the year that she'd known Steven, the two of them had never shared an intimate meal together that had been prepared by one of them. Oh, they'd eaten together, but it had always been something delivered by hotel room service or served in some out-of-the-way restaurant where they wouldn't run into anyone they knew.

"Penny for your thoughts," Steven said as he handed her the sauce pan to dry.

"I was thinking that I've shared more home-cooked meals with you here in Montana than I did all of this past year in Boston."

"Not by my choice," he reminded her.

It was true. Steven had pleaded with her time and again to spend the evening with him at his apartment or to allow him to spend it at her place. And always she'd refused, fearful that someone might see them together at his apartment and unwilling to risk her family seeing him at hers. "You know why I insisted on keeping our relationship a secret," she said defensively.

"Yes, I knew. But I never agreed with it. Anyway, there's no point in worrying about someone finding out our secret now. They're all going to know soon enough. And the longer we put off telling them, the more difficult it's going to be." He dried his hands and hung up the dish towel. "We have nothing to be ashamed of, Maria. Nothing."

"I'm not ashamed." And she wasn't. She was simply scared—scared of disappointing and hurting her family, of letting them down. Scared of disappointing Steven. Scared that she would put her baby in danger.

He turned to her, held her shoulders. "Then say that you'll marry me and we'll go to see our families together and tell them about the baby."

"Meow." Sophia rubbed up against her ankles, then began to wind her body around Steven's legs, meowing all the while.

Seizing on the interruption, Maria said, "I need to feed Sophia."

Steven's mouth hardened, but he released her without pressing her for an answer. "I'll feed her for you," he said.

"Thanks."

"It'd probably be a good idea to get a weather update," he suggested.

"I'll check the radio in the den."

He nodded. "As soon as I feed Sophia, I'll fix us some hot chocolate."

"That sounds great."

"Your timing sucks," he muttered to the cat as he walked over to the counter and took the leftover cut-up chicken he'd set aside earlier and dumped it into her dish.

Smiling at this soft side of Steven, Maria exited the kitchen and headed for the den. She flipped on the radio and after listening to an update about closing roads and expectations of more snow, she switched it off and popped Faith Hill's newest release into the CD player. As Faith began to sing about love and heartache, Maria walked over to the window. Pushing the drapes aside, she stared out into the darkness at a world blanketed in white. Isolated as they were, it was so easy to forget about Boston, about her and Steven's families, about the problems they would soon have to face. So far removed from everything and everyone, she could almost pretend they were a normal couple in love and expecting a baby, that they could share a life together just as Steven claimed.

"Anything new on the weather?"

Releasing the drape, Maria turned around and watched as Steven entered the room carrying a tray. "Just more snow and some road closures. It was depressing, so I put on some music."

"Ready for that hot chocolate?" he asked, setting the tray onto the floor in front of the fireplace. He knelt down beside it.

"Don't you think the couch would be more comfortable?"

"Probably," he said as he reached over, grabbed the throw pillows from the love seat and tossed them down onto the floor next to the tray. "But I doubt that the skewers will reach that far."

"The skewers?" she repeated even as she sat down onto the floor across from him.

"For the marshmallows." He held up a long wooden stick with a marshmallow on the end of it. "Evidently you were never a Boy Scout."

Maria laughed. "No. And I wasn't a Girl Scout either."

"Then you've obviously missed out on one of the rituals of childhood."

"Is that so?" she countered, enjoying the easy banter.

"Absolutely. But not to worry, I'll teach you. I'm a master when it comes to roasting marshmallows."

"My, my. Aren't you the humble one?" she teased.

"Humility is overrated," he told her. "Now pay attention. Observe the angle of the wrist," he instructed as he held the marshmallow over the fire.

"Looks pretty simple to me."

Giving her a dismissive look, he rotated the skewer slowly, allowing the flames to lick at the white puff until it turned a pale golden brown. After he removed it from the fire, he blew on the marshmallow a second or two, then held it up to her lips. "Prepare to be seduced."

She was seduced. Not just by the warm, sweet, gooey marshmallow but by Steven as he fed her the tasty treats. "Enough," she said laughing after he had fed her several of the roasted marshmallows. "I swear if I eat another bite, I'll explode. As it is, I'm not sure I'll be able to get up I'm so fat."

"You look fine to me."

"You've got to be kidding. I look like I've swallowed a basketball. Maybe you'd better schedule an eye exam when you get back to Boston."

"There's not a thing wrong with my eyes. I've always thought you were beautiful. But there's a glow, a radiance about you now that makes you even more beautiful than ever," he said.

"Thank you," she murmured, not sure what to say.

"No need to thank me. It's the truth." Removing another marshmallow from the skewer, he ate half of it and offered the remainder to her.

Maria opened her mouth, allowed him to feed her the other piece. Her teeth grazed the pad of his finger and she swallowed hard as his eyes darkened to smoke. "No more," she told him, looking away.

"You've got a little bit of marshmallow right here," he told her, indicating the corner of her mouth.

Maria licked at it with her tongue, felt her pulse jump as Steven watched her with an intensity that was palpable.

"Hang on a second," he said, his voice a deep rumble. Leaning closer, he flicked his finger near the edge of her mouth and then brought it to his lips.

Suddenly heat that had nothing to do with the fire spilled through Maria, igniting desire in her and awakening a need that had remained dormant for months. Once her pregnancy started to show, she'd been too shocked and worried to allow herself to be with him for fear he would find out her secret. Since she'd fled to Montana, she hadn't wanted to remember what it was like to make love with him. But she remembered now. And the memory set off an ache inside her that made her cheeks heat and her palms dampen. Afraid she would do or say something foolish, she reached for her cup of chocolate. She drank deeply and tried to get a handle on her emotions and the desire that Steven had set off inside her.

"Maria, look at me."

When she did as he'd asked, he removed the cup from her fingers and set it aside. Then everything seemed to move in slow motion as he took her face in his hands and began to lower his head. She registered the gleam in his blue eyes, the dark shadow along his jaw, the slight parting of his lips. And at the touch of his mouth, she trembled and closed her eyes.

He kissed her. Gently. Softly. Slowly. He kissed her as though they had all the time in the world. As though there was no outside world or families or problems, only them.

"You taste like chocolate," he whispered, sliding his tongue along the seam of her lips. "And marshmallows. Sweet. So sweet," he continued, seducing her with his mouth, making love to her with kiss after kiss. Her head was filled with his scent, with his taste, with his touch.

He lifted his head a fraction, angled it and kissed her again. And with each kiss, all the reasons she'd given herself why she couldn't be with Steven began to fade. As though in a dream, she fell under the spell of Steven's kisses, like a swimmer going under for the third time.

You should stop.

She heard the voice whispering in her head and ignored it. She didn't want to stop. She wanted Steven to go on kissing her. He'd never kissed her like this before. Never with such exquisite patience. In the past, their time together had been filled with stolen moments and there was always a sense of urgency to their lovemaking. But not now. Now there were only slow, tender kisses that went on and on and on, until the ache inside her sharpened into hurt.

Pulling her mouth free, she sucked in a breath and

stared up at him. "Touch me," she pleaded. "I want to feel your hands on me."

Steven's eyes flashed, went even darker. And for a moment Maria felt a thrill of feminine power. But then his hand was on her breast. And she could no longer think. She could scarcely breathe as he squeezed and kneaded her sensitive flesh. When he lowered his head and closed his mouth over her sweater, Maria gasped. The moist heat of his mouth suckling her through the fabric was erotic and only fed the desire already running rampant inside her.

"I want to see you," he whispered, his voice raw, his eyes filled with a savage hunger that made her pulse leap.

Fearing her voice would fail her, she nodded. As though in a dream, she watched him through half-slitted lids as he pushed up her sweater. The firelight shimmered off his dark hair and she slid her fingers through it. When he unclasped the hook at the front of her bra, his fingertips brushed her midriff. Sucking in a breath, Maria waited. Then what seemed an eternity later, his tongue circled her nipple. She gasped. Closing her eyes, she arched her back.

Steven took her into his mouth. Taking his time, he suckled, kissed, laved first one breast, then the other. With each touch of his lips, each stroke of his tongue, liquid heat pooled between her thighs. And finally when he closed his teeth around her nipple, gave it a gentle nip, Maria bit down on her lower lip to keep from crying out.

As though he sensed her need, Steven slid his hand down her hip, along the length of her skirt and beneath it. Then he smoothed his way back up the inside of her leg. When he reached the edge of her panties, his voice was ragged as he asked, "Do you want me to stop? God knows I don't want to, but I will if it's what you want."

"No," she managed to get the word out from a throat dry with need. "I don't want you to stop."

He made some sound deep in his throat and then he kissed her again. And as he kissed her, his hand found its way beneath the edge of her panties and he eased first one finger, then another inside her. He began to stroke her. Slowly moving in and out, in and out. And all the while he kept kissing her. More of those same painstakingly slow kisses that were driving her crazy. He slid his fingers inside, nearly withdrew, then entered her again.

Maria tore her mouth free, clutched his shoulders as she felt herself near flash point. "Steven," she cried out as he entered her again, stroked that sensitive spot over and over until finally she exploded. She bucked beneath his hand, cried out again and then shattered into a thousand points of light.

Steven held her close, drinking in Maria's cries as another orgasm ripped through her. Her response had his own desire spiking. When she went limp in his arms seconds later, he eased her back down onto the cushions. He kissed her gently. And after smoothing down her skirt, he tucked her against him, contented himself to simply hold her. Even though the ache in his groin would probably keep him awake for a good part of the night, he found some satisfaction in knowing that he had given her the sexual release.

She stirred beside him, her hip nudging his shaft, and Steven bit off a groan. It was definitely going to be a long night, he decided, sucking in a breath.

"Steven?"

"Yeah?" he managed to get out, still trying to temper his desire.

"Aren't you… Aren't we…"

She shifted again and this time, he did groan aloud.

She eased up to her elbow, looked down at him. "Why did you stop? Why didn't you make love with me?"

Steven reached up, touched her cheek. "I did make love with you."

"No. You made love *to* me—not *with* me. There's a difference. I… There was satisfaction for me, but none for you."

"There was a lot of satisfaction for me," he insisted and meant every word. "Seeing you, knowing that I could give you that was incredibly satisfying."

"I don't see how you can say that when you didn't… When you didn't experience what I did."

"I experienced it through you. Giving you pleasure is what I wanted."

"And that's enough for you?"

"Yes," he told her even though his body swore the word to be a lie. He did want her, but his love for her was greater than his desire, and he refused to put her or their baby at risk to appease his physical hunger. There would be time enough later, after the baby was born and they were living as husband and wife. Because of one thing he was sure—he was not going to go back to Boston without Maria and her promise to be his wife.

"I see," she said, her expression falling. "I guess I should have realized that you…that I…" She whooshed out a breath and gave him a self-deprecating smile. "I mean, I could hardly expect you to be overcome with passion when I look like I swallowed a watermelon and my—"

"Don't," Steven fired back, furious with her for believing he had rejected her and with himself for not realizing that she would. "You're beautiful. And you're sexy as hell and I want you so badly right now I can hardly breathe." And to prove his point, he reached for her hand, pressed it against the bulge in his slacks.

She looked up at him, her brows creased. "Then why did you—? Why didn't you—"

"Because I didn't want to hurt you and I was afraid it might hurt the baby."

"Oh, Steven," she said in a rush and hugged him.

He wrapped his arms around her, held her against him. "There'll be lots of other times, Maria. I can wait until after the baby's born."

She eased away from him. "But you don't have to wait. I mean, it's all right if we make love. It won't hurt me or the baby." When he hesitated, she kissed him and whispered against his mouth, "Make love with me, Steven."

Steven hesitated.

She licked his mouth with her tongue, nipped his bottom lip and repeated, "Make love with me."

His body, already tense and aching from exercising restraint, went down for the count. "I'd have to be a saint to refuse. And we both know I'm no saint," he told her.

"I don't want a saint. I want you. Only you."

He nearly attacked her mouth, caught himself just in time and forced himself to keep it slow, to keep it easy. Though it cost him, he took his time undressing her slowly, marveling at the changes in her body since the last time he'd seen her naked. Her breasts were fuller, the nipples a deeper rose that pouted and begged for him to taste them, to kiss them. He obliged.

He sloped his hands down her waist, her hips, and was surprised they remained so small. He kissed the swell of her belly, the inside of her thighs. Moving between her legs, he opened her to his mouth. He tasted her. He explored her. And using his tongue and his teeth, he brought her up, took her over one peak and then another. All the while his own desire sharpened. The blood in his veins ran thick and hot with need. And when he could wait no longer, he stripped off his jeans and boxers and moved between her thighs.

He braced himself above her, determined not to let her bear any of his weight. "I'll try to be gentle," he promised, aware of how small she was despite the pregnancy.

"I'm not made of glass, Steven. I won't break."

"I know that," he said. "But we're going to take this slow and easy."

"Slow and easy," she repeated and closed her fist around him.

Steven sucked in a breath. His vision blurred and before he realized what was happening, it was Maria pushing him down to the pillows. Maria climbing astride him.

"Maria, you don't—" He swore, both excited and alarmed by the look in her eyes. "Easy," he hissed as she started to lower herself onto his shaft.

"I know slow and easy," she repeated his words to him and began to move.

She kept her word. She took things slow. She took things easy. Rocking back and forth, back and forth, taking him deeper and deeper inside her. Pleasuring herself, pleasuring him with each stroke, with each cant of her hips. Steven filled his hands with her breasts, shaped and molded her hips. What he felt for this woman went beyond lust, beyond desire, he admitted. He loved her with every fiber of his being, with his very soul. Nothing, no one would keep them apart, he vowed.

Steven arched up to taste her breasts and the movement drove him deeper inside her and nearly drove him over the edge. All the while, Maria continued the slow canting of her hips, pushing him closer and closer to the edge. She leaned all the way forward, sprawling her naked body atop him and spearing her fingers through his hair. Then she kissed him again, assaulting his mouth, and when she tore her lips free, the glint in her eyes stole his breath.

"You did say slow and easy, right?"

"Right," he said, nearly choking out the word. Unable to resist, he swept a hand over her naked body and reveled in the moan that escaped her lips. She was all soft, pale limbs and big dark eyes, a wood nymph come to life. And he had never seen anything more beautiful, he thought.

She continued to move atop him, gradually increasing the tempo. Then her body tensed. She closed her eyes, tipped back her head and arched her back. "Steven," she cried out his name on a gasp.

He gripped her hips, held on to her and lifted his own hips, driving himself up and into her fast. Faster. Faster still. And then the orgasm ripped through her. She trembled, her feminine muscles quivered around him. Steven groaned with the effort it took to hold back his own release and draw out the pleasure for them both.

"Steven," she called out, reaching for him as she climaxed again.

Unable to wait any longer, he followed her over the edge and into the storm. And suddenly, the house went dark.

* * *

Sprawled atop Steven in front of the fireplace, her body flushed with sexual satisfaction, Maria couldn't work up enough energy to move, let alone to find her clothes and redress. For the moment, all thoughts of Boston and their problems seemed far, far away.

"Are you all right?"

"I think so. I'll let you know as soon as I can move again," she murmured lazily.

He chuckled, the sound a deep rumble beneath her ear. "You do realize the power went out, don't you?"

"Is that what happened? I thought the world exploded."

"You're very good for my ego, Ms. Barone," he said, a smile in his voice.

"You're ego doesn't need any boosting, Mr. Conti. You're the most self-assured person I know."

"Maybe in most things," he said, pressing a kiss to her head. "But not when it comes to you."

Moved by his admission, Maria snuggled closer, breathed in his scent. And when he stroked his fingers down her spine, she shivered.

"Cold?"

"A little," she admitted. Now that the heat of their lovemaking was over, she was becoming all too aware of her naked state and the waning fire.

"Give me a few minutes and I'll see what I can do to warm you up."

Maria smiled against his chest, then slid off of him and onto her side. She glanced around for her clothes, but before she could retrieve them, Steven had snagged the afghan from the end of the chair. He draped it over her.

"Better?"

"Yes. Thanks," she said and burrowed beneath the

coverlet while Steven got up and began dragging on his jeans with the lithe movements of a leopard, all sinew and rippling muscles. Enamored with the sight of him, she couldn't help hoping that he made good on his promise to warm her up again. Surprised by her thoughts, she looked away as he pulled on his sweater.

"Stay put," he told her as he shoved into his boots. He tossed another log onto the fire.

"Where are you going?"

"To see about switching over to the generator."

"I'll go with you," she told him and started to get up.

Steven immediately knelt beside her, blocking her path. "I'd rather you stayed inside where it's warm. That way you can warm me up when I get back."

Maria flushed and was about to protest when he gave her a deep, toe-curling kiss. Lifting his head, he said, "Think of the baby. You don't want to risk getting a cold or slipping in the snow, do you? Especially not while we're stranded here in a blizzard."

"I've heard this before," she reminded him.

"And it's still true. For now, it's just the two of us and I want to make sure you're safe."

But it wouldn't be just the two of them for much longer, Maria thought as she watched Steven head outdoors. Sooner or later, the snow would end. The roads would open up. And the two of them would no longer be isolated from the rest of the world. These idyllic moments and this magical time of pretending that she and Steven were two normal people in love would have to come to an end.

The end came two mornings later with the ringing of Steven's cell phone. Although Maria attempted to leave the room to give him some privacy, he motioned for her to stay. But she knew from his expression and the tension in his body that the news wasn't good. "All right. The roads reopened this morning and my cell phone's obviously working again. I'll leave on the next available flight to Boston. In the meantime, keep me informed if you find out anything else."

"What is it?" Maria asked. "What's happened?"

"That was Ethan Mallory," he said, referring to the detective the Contis had hired following her family's accusations of sabotage at Baronessa Gelateria. Mallory was also the same detective who had subsequently been working to locate both Bianca and Derrick following the kidnappings.

"Has he found your sister and Derrick?"

"Not yet." He held Maria at arm's length, stared into her eyes. "But there's no longer any question that Derrick is responsible for the arson at Baronessa's."

As much as she hadn't wanted to believe her own cousin could do such a thing, she'd known that the evidence all pointed to him. "What about the kidnappings? Karen said it was beginning to look like Derrick might have staged the whole thing."

"That's why Ethan called. Your cousin Emily went to see a hypnotist. She's remembered things and from the information she's given them, the Feds have been able to link the ransom note back to Derrick."

"Poor Emily," Maria said, her thoughts turning to her cousin. "This must all be so hard on her."

"Let's not forget my sister. Bianca's the innocent party in all this."

Maria flinched, the sharpness in Steven's tone slapping at her like an icy wind. She hugged her arms about herself. "I'm sorry," she said. "I wasn't making light of what's happened to Bianca. It's just that as Derrick's sister, Emily can't be taking this well. Of course, I can't even begin to imagine how much worse this all has to be for you and your family."

Steven sighed. He rubbed the back of his neck. "This whole thing has been a nightmare for everyone. I'm sorry I snapped at you."

"You're entitled."

"No, I'm not," he insisted. "This isn't your fault. None of this has anything to do with you."

"It has everything to do with me, Steven. Derrick's my cousin."

"Just because you share the same last name doesn't make you responsible for his actions."

"I'm not so sure your family will see the distinction," she pointed out.

"You let me worry about my family. In the meantime, I'm going to have to go back to Boston."

"Of course," she said, already missing him and regretting their return to the real world. "I understand."

"I don't want to go back by myself. Come with me."

"I don't think that's a good idea," she told him.

"Maria," he began and reached for her.

Maria stepped away. "Besides, even if I wanted to, I couldn't go right now and leave Sophia alone. Who would take care of her while Louis and Magdalene are away?"

"I thought Magdalene told you that Louis's father was okay now and that they'd be leaving Billings tomorrow or the next day?"

"Yes, she did," Maria admitted. Since she had related the earlier conversation to Steven, she could hardly deny it. "But that means they won't get back here until late tomorrow at the earliest."

"Then Sophia will only be alone for a little while. Cats are very self-sufficient, Maria. If we put out plenty of food and water for her, Sophia will do just fine until the Calderones get home."

"But they're depending on me to take care of her for them," Maria argued. Even though she knew he was right, the prospect of returning to Boston set off an avalanche of nerves. "Louis and Magdalene have been very good to me. I don't want to let them down."

"You wouldn't be letting them down," Steven insisted. "I'm sure if we called them and explained what's happened and that we have to return to Boston, they'll understand."

"I don't know, Steven."

He moved toward her, took her hands in his and looked into her eyes. "Please, Maria, I need you. Come with me."

Maria hesitated, overwhelmed by the thought of facing her family, of possibly facing Steven's family as well. Although she had resigned herself to the fact that she would have to tell her own family the truth, she hadn't expected it to be so soon. How would they react to the news about her and Steven? About the baby?

"If you won't come for me…for us," he amended, "then come for my sister."

"How will my coming to Boston help Bianca?"

"Because you can talk to Emily. She trusts you. If she knows anything at all about where her brother's hiding, she'll tell you."

"But you said Emily was cooperating with that detective your family hired and that she'd been to see a hypnotist."

"She is cooperating with Ethan, and seeing the hypnotist did help. But not all of the pieces have come together yet and we're running out of time. Derrick's already tried to burn down your family's plant and kidnapped Bianca. There's no telling what he'll do next. The man's not stable, Maria. Surely you realize that.''

"Yes, I realize it.'' And it was the truth. Unlike her relationships with her other cousins, she and Derrick had never been close. She'd long ago chalked it up to Derrick's penchant for grand schemes to make it big instead of working hard to achieve success. Of course, it hadn't helped that his twin, Daniel, had been so dynamic and had succeeded in everything he did. Next to Daniel, Derrick had paled in comparison—in both personality and in his achievements. She remembered all too clearly now how he'd become even more bitter when he'd been overlooked for key corporate jobs at Baronessa.

"Then you also realize that he's dangerous?''

Maria recalled the venom in Derrick's voice when he'd congratulated her on becoming manager of the gelateria and told her that he hoped someday she'd get everything she deserved. A chill raced down Maria's spine. "Yes," she said.

"It won't be long before he figures out that the Feds have tied the ransom note to him. Once he does, Bianca's going to be in even greater danger. We've got to find him and we've got to do it soon.'' He paused, met her gaze with serious blue eyes. "Please, will you come with me?''

"All right. I'll come. On one condition.''

"What?''

"You have to promise that you won't tell anyone about us or the baby until I say so.''

"All right. But don't you think it's going to be difficult to hide your pregnancy from your family?'' he pointed out.

"Except for Emily, I don't intend to see my family. At least not right away."

Steven's mouth hardened, but he remained silent.

"I know I have to tell them, Steven. And I will. I promise. But first I want to resolve this mess with Derrick and make sure that Bianca's okay."

Maybe then she'd be able to figure out how she was going to break the news to her family that she loved Steven Conti and was expecting his baby and wanted to marry him. More importantly, she'd have to decide whether to face Lucia Conti and risk the wrath of the Conti curse.

Nine

"**S**he's late," Steven told Maria later that evening as they waited in her office at Baronessa's headquarters. "Maybe you should call her again."

"She's only ten minutes late. Don't worry. Emily will be here."

Impatient, Steven prowled about the room. When he glanced at his watch for the third time in as many minutes, he tried not to second-guess his idea to have Maria question her cousin, nor wonder whether it would work. According to Mallory, both he and the Feds had already questioned the woman. And while she'd been helpful, she hadn't been able to give them anything that would lead them to her brother. No doubt both the detective and the Feds would see his having Maria speak to her cousin as more interference on his part.

Tough! Bianca was his sister, dammit. He couldn't just keep waiting around for them to find out where Derrick had taken her. By the time they did, it might be too late. Just the thought of something happening to his sister left a sick feeling in his gut, and Steven did his best to temper that fear. He would find Bianca, he promised himself. He just wished he'd thought of asking Maria to help him sooner. But then, he had been so stunned to discover Maria was pregnant and so intent on getting her to see reason that he hadn't been thinking clearly. Maybe if he'd been more focused on finding his sister than on his own worries with Maria, they would have found Bianca by now.

"Steven, Emily will be here soon," Maria assured him.

"So you keep saying."

"She will. I just hope she gets here before you wear a hole in my carpet."

Steven stopped pacing, glanced over at her.

"Try to relax," she urged.

"I can't," he told her honestly. He rubbed the back of his neck, felt the knots of tension there. "I can't stop thinking about Bianca, how frightened she must be."

"I'm sorry. I wish there was something I could do."

"You're doing it. Or you will be once your cousin gets here. *If* she gets here." At the stern look Maria shot him, Steven sighed. "I know I'm being impatient. It's just that Bianca will be depending on me. I've always been there whenever she's needed me, and she probably wonders why I haven't rescued her already."

"You'll find her," Maria told him. "You found me, didn't you?"

"You weren't kidnapped and taken away against your will," he pointed out.

"You're right. I wasn't. But I didn't want to be found and you found me anyway."

"I don't think I can count on your cousin slipping up and using a credit card," Steven informed her. "If I only had an idea where he might have taken her, where to look for her."

"Try not to worry. If Bianca is anything at all like her brother, she's a lot tougher than you think."

"She's not like me. She's fragile and trusting and…" He thought of his sister in some dingy warehouse, bound and terrified, and a crazed Derrick Barone threatening her. "And so help me, if that bastard has done anything to her, I'll—" He bit off the rest. Swearing, he turned away.

"I'm sorry."

Steven sucked in a breath. He scrubbed a hand down his face and turned around to face Maria once more. "No, I'm the one who's sorry. I had no right lashing out at you like that."

"You're entitled. I can only imagine what you must be feeling. If it were one of my sisters being held by a Conti, I'd be angry, too. I just hope…I hope you're right about my talking to Emily, that it will help you to find Bianca."

"It will," he assured her and prayed to God he was right. He forced himself to think about other times when he'd been faced with impossible odds and had triumphed. The start-up and success of his company. His and Maria falling in love and creating a child together in spite of the bitter feud between their families. Getting Maria to return to Boston with him today had been another major hurdle. Granted, she hadn't agreed to marry him yet, but that was a detail he would work on once he found Bianca.

"Would you like something to drink while we wait? There's some bottled water and cold drinks in the re-

frigerator over there by the counter,'' Maria told him.
''And I think there's some wine in the fridge in the
boardroom.''

''No thanks.''

''I think I'll get myself some water,'' she said, and
standing, she walked over to the refrigerator.

As she did so, Steven took in the surroundings. Although Maria had insisted that they turn on only a single
lamp in the office, there was enough light for him to
note that the room's decor reflected her. She'd chosen
neutral tones of ivory and sand, then added dashes of
color with plants, flowers and paintings. There was nothing splashy about the room—just an understated ele-
gance and beauty with surprising touches that prevented
it from being merely another nicely decorated office. Instead it was an intriguing place that dared you to remain
immune to its charm. Just like the woman who occupied
it, he thought as Maria made her way back to the desk
with the bottle of water. She wore a black turtleneck and
slate-colored jacket, with a silver pendant hanging from
the chain around her neck that glinted in the light as she
sat down. She sipped at the water while idly clenching
and unclenching the pen in her hand.

Nerves, he realized. He didn't blame her. His own
nerves were stretched rather thin. And he couldn't get
Mallory's last words out of his head.

''I'll be honest with you, Conti. From my conversa-
tions with Emily, I think the guy's a loose cannon. The
longer this drags on, the more likely he is to blow.''

And if Derrick Barone blew, the one who would suffer
would be Bianca. Guilt and worry pummeled at him like
fists. He had to do something, anything, to find his sister.
''What in the devil could be taking her so long?'' he

snapped. And as if in answer, the elevator bell dinged, announcing the car's arrival on the floor.

"That must be Emily," Maria said.

About time, Steven thought as he waited anxiously for the other woman to enter Maria's office. Only she wasn't alone. But before he could demand to know who the tall, sandy-haired man with her was, Emily was rushing past him to Maria.

"Maria! I can't believe you're here. Where have you been? Why are we meeting here? And what—" The other woman broke off the hug, stepped back and stared at her cousin's protruding belly, then back at her face.

"I'm pregnant," Maria explained.

"But how? Who?" Suddenly she whipped her attention over to Steven. "Oh."

"I'm the baby's father," Steven said as he walked over and put his arm around Maria's shoulders. "I intend to marry your cousin with or without your or my family's approvals," Steven continued, feeling the need to make his position perfectly clear.

"I see," she murmured, her eyes flicking from Steven's face back to her cousin's.

"Except for Karen and now you and Shane," Maria said, directing her attention to the man standing beside Emily with a protective arm about her, "no one in either of our families knows about the baby or us yet," Maria told them. "It's why I asked you to meet me here and not tell anyone. I'd appreciate it if you didn't say anything."

"We won't," Emily assured her. "Will we, Shane?"

"Mum's the word," Shane replied. "Please accept my congratulations. You, too," he added with a nod in Steven's direction.

"I don't believe we've met," Steven said pointedly. He extended his hand. "Steven Conti."

"Shane Cummings. I was the fireman on the scene of the plant fire where Emily was injured," he explained as he shook hands. "Conti as in Antonio Conti's restaurant? The Contis who put the curse on the Barones?"

"That's right," Steven said defensively.

"Great Italian food at Antonio's," the muscled man with the friendly smile said. "I treat myself to the manicotti every few months."

"I'm sure my family appreciates it," Steven responded. "It was my understanding that the arson investigation was closed, and it was determined that Derrick Barone was responsible."

"That's right. But I decided that I wanted to investigate Emily more thoroughly. We're getting married."

Steven couldn't help but envy the pair who were so obviously in love and had no qualms about the world and everyone else knowing it. Since his own relationship with Maria had been conducted in secrecy, they'd never enjoyed the luxury of simply being two people in love. But that was all going to change, he promised himself. But first, he had to find Bianca. "I hate to cut this short, but we don't have a lot of time. Emily, did Maria tell you why she asked you to meet her here?"

The petite dark-haired woman with the striking resemblance to Maria nodded. "She said she needed my help."

"Steven thinks... We think," Maria amended as she looked up at him beside her. She caught his hand, squeezed it before focusing again on her cousin. "We're hoping that maybe if you talk to me, that you might be able to remember something that will help us find where Derrick is holding Bianca."

Emily's expression fell. Her brown eyes were filled with regret as she looked at Steven. "I'm not sure what I can tell you that I haven't already told Ethan Mallory and the federal agents. Please believe me, if I had any idea where Derrick might be, I swear I'd tell you."

"I know you would," Maria told her cousin. Moving away from Steven, she reached out and took her cousin's hands. "Will you at least talk to us? Maybe if you tell me what you've told the agents and the detective, it might spark something that you've forgotten."

"I don't see how putting her through this again will help," Shane informed her.

"It's all right, Shane. I want to help. It's the least I can do since my brother is the one responsible. Where do you want me to begin?"

"Why don't we start with the week of the fire...."

"I'm sorry," Emily said nearly thirty minutes later after recounting the days leading up to and following the fire at the plant. She was exhausted and speaking of her brother, accepting the fact that her own flesh and blood could deliberately attempt to destroy and sabotage their family's business, hurt beyond belief.

"This isn't getting us anywhere," Steven said impatiently. "What about before the fire? Can you remember seeing your brother with anyone? Or maybe hearing him make plans to meet at a place that seemed odd to you?"

"I think Emily's had enough of your questions," Shane said, standing up from his seat at the table around which the four of them had gathered. "Let's go, Emily."

Steven swore. "Her damn brother's got my sister, pal," Steven fired back. "She's our only hope of finding her."

"I'm sorry about your sister. But Emily's been

through enough. She's done answering your questions,'' Shane countered.

Before Steven could erupt again and the testosterone escalated any further between the two men, Emily said, ''It's all right, Shane. I'm okay.''

''No, you're not,'' he argued. He stooped down beside her. ''You don't owe them anything. You don't have to put yourself through this again.''

''Yes, I do. It's obvious my brother's not well. Somehow, I missed all the signs,'' she said, regret filling her heart. How could she not have realized that her brother had begun to spin out of control? She swiped a tear from the corner of her eye. ''I want to find Derrick just as much as they do. I want…I need to try.''

''You're sure you're up to this?'' Shane asked her.

The love and concern in his blue-green eyes warmed her, gave her strength. She squeezed the fingers holding her own. ''I'm sure.''

''Thank you,'' Steven said and resumed his seat.

Emily nodded, recognizing that this was as difficult for him as it was for her. Maybe more so. ''What else do you want to know?''

''Maybe Steven's on the right track,'' Maria began. ''You said that you'd recognized the name of a competitor who had called Derrick.''

''That's right. Snowcream. I told Uncle Carlo about it.''

''But what about before then? Can you think of anything else or someone else he might have been seeing or talking to that you found strange?''

Emily concentrated, tried to remember back to the months before the fire, before she'd discovered her own brother was willing to sell the secret recipes for profit. And then she recalled waiting in Derrick's office for him so that the two of them could go out to lunch and discuss an anniversary gift and party for their parents....

Emily tapped her foot impatiently as she glanced at her watch. Typical Derrick, she thought, miffed that her brother was late once again. She frowned, wondered why Derrick couldn't be more considerate. His arriving late yesterday at the company meeting hadn't sat well with Maria or anyone else.

But then it probably wasn't easy for Derrick who felt he was always being compared to his twin. He was wrong, of course. The only one who'd ever compared him to Daniel was Derrick himself. Emily sighed and wished, not for the first time, that she understood her brother.

She glanced at her watch again. Perhaps she should try to reach Derrick on his cell phone, she decided, and was just about to call him when the phone on his desk rang. Since she knew Derrick's assistant was at lunch, she grabbed the phone and answered, "Derrick Barone's desk."

"Is Derrick there?" a woman asked in a breathy voice that sounded suspiciously like Amber's, the wife of Derrick's best friend.

"Amber?"

"I'll take that," Derrick said, snatching the phone from Emily's fingers.

"I know, baby. I miss you, too. But I got tied up with business and couldn't get away," he said to the woman on the phone. "Yeah, me too. But I promise I'll make it up to you later." He paused, glanced at his watch. "Why don't we meet at the usual place say around four?"

"Was that Amber Hopkins?" Emily asked when he hung up the phone.

"Of course not. Why would I be making plans to meet Larry's wife?"

"That's what I was wondering myself."

"Obviously, it wasn't Amber," Derrick told her.

She wanted to believe him, hated that she had such suspicions about her own brother. Still, there had been something almost sinister in Derrick's eyes when he'd spoken to the woman. It was the same look she'd seen when he'd borrowed Daniel's car and wrecked it. He'd claimed it was an accident, that someone had run him off the road. But Emily hadn't quite believed him. *"It certainly sounded like Amber to me."*

"Well, it wasn't her," Derrick assured her.

"Then who was she?"

"What is this? Twenty questions? She's just someone that I'm seeing," he snapped. *"Now are you ready to go to lunch or not?"*

"I'm ready." Even though she didn't believe that her brother was being honest with her, she decided to let it go.

"I thought we'd try that new place that opened up down the block," Derrick told her and started to hustle her toward the door. As he did so, her purse caught the stack of letters on the corner of his desk and sent them tumbling to the floor.

"Oh, look what I've done!" She stooped down to pick up the scattered letters.

"Just leave it," he ordered. *"My secretary will take care of it when she gets back from lunch."*

"I will do no such thing," she informed him and began gathering up the envelopes and letters.

Grumbling, her brother squatted down beside her and starting swiping the mail up from the floor.

Emily picked up another letter and noted the addressee wasn't her brother. "Who's Anthony Woodward?" she asked, reading the name on the envelope.

"Beats me," Derrick said and snatched the envelope from her. "His mail must have been delivered to me by mistake."

Emily finished gathering the mail and couldn't help noticing that Derrick had slipped the envelope into his briefcase. Standing, she returned the stack of letters to her brother's desk.

Derrick did the same and then asked sarcastically, "Satisfied now?"

Emily nodded, although the truth was she was far from satisfied.

"Then why don't we grab some lunch and talk about the anniversary party?"

"Emily? Emily?" Maria's voice finally penetrated. "You still with us?"

"Yes. I just remembered something that happened a few months ago," she began and related the incident in Derrick's office. "I'm not sure what it means, but I was pretty sure Derrick was lying to me about the woman, and something about the whole thing with the mail bothered me."

"Does the name Anthony Woodward mean anything to you?" Steven asked.

"No. I never heard of him."

"Wait a minute," Maria said, her voice excited, her eyes bright. "Emily, what was Aunt Sandra's maiden name?"

"Oh my God, you're right. Woodward is my mother's

maiden name. And Anthony...Anthony is Derrick's middle name."

Steven whipped out his cell phone and punched in some numbers. "Operator, I need a listing for Anthony Woodward and the address, too, if you have it."

Emily waited, her heart pounding in her chest. A part of her wanted it to be Derrick, while another part of her prayed that they were all wrong. Despite all the evidence that pointed to her brother as an arsonist and saboteur, she didn't want to believe him capable of this. But as Steven jotted down the phone number and address, Emily knew deep inside that Derrick was indeed capable of staging his own kidnapping and taking Bianca Conti as hostage.

"Got it," Steven said as he ended the call and held up the slip of paper with the information. Grabbing Maria, he kissed her quick on the mouth. "Thank you for agreeing to come back, for agreeing to help me," he whispered.

"You're welcome," Maria told him, and Emily didn't miss the love and longing in her cousin's expression. "But the one you should really be thanking is Emily."

Steven marched over to her and said, "Excuse me, Cummings." Then he took her hands into his own and pressed a gentle kiss to her forehead. "Thank you," he said, his blue eyes bright. "I can't imagine how difficult this was for you and I know I'll never be able to repay you for what you've done. My sister owes you her life, Emily. So do I."

She nodded. "You don't owe me anything. I just hope you're right. That you'll find your sister at that address and that she's...that she's okay."

"Thanks." He paused, his expression suddenly solemn. "I've got to go. Maria," he said turning back to her cousin, "maybe you could go home with Emily and Shane and I'll—"

"I'm going with you."

"But—"

"I'm going with you, Steven," Maria said firmly.

"You might as well give up, Conti," Shane told him. "If there's one thing I've learned about these Barone women, it's that they make up their own minds."

Steven relented. "All right. Let's go."

"Thanks again," Maria told her, hugging her close. "Take care of my cousin, Shane."

"You can count on it."

"Steven," Emily called out as they started to leave.

He paused, turned back to look at her and waited.

"Derrick has—" She swallowed, tried again. "He used to have a gun."

He nodded. "I appreciate the warning. I'll be careful."

"And please," she said to their retreating backs, "please try not to hurt my brother."

Maria's heart ached for her cousin as they left the office building and headed to the garage for Steven's car. How would she feel if it were one of her brothers who had betrayed their family? Suddenly her stomach sank and she couldn't help wondering if everyone would think her a traitor when they learned about Steven and the baby.

"I know the area where Derrick's got the apartment," Steven said tightly. "It's probably going to take us a good thirty to forty minutes to get there."

"Are you going to call the FBI and Ethan and tell them what we found out?"

"Not yet," Steven told her as they approached the car.

"But I thought you told Ethan that you'd call if we found out anything."

"I did and I will call him." He unlocked Maria's door. "Just not yet."

Maria narrowed her eyes. "What are you planning to do?"

"I'm going to go to the apartment, *then* I'm going to call Mallory. He can tell the feds. That way it'll be too late for them to order me to stay away." He shut her door, walked around to the driver's side and slid behind the wheel.

"I don't guess there's any point in my asking you to let the authorities handle it?" she asked as she buckled her seat belt.

"No. Bianca's my sister. I have to do this." He started the engine, looked over at her. "But I wish you'd re-consider and let me take you someplace where you'll be safe until this is over."

"I'm going with you."

"Dammit, Maria. You heard Emily. Derrick's got a gun. The man's dangerous. I don't want you putting yourself and our baby at risk. If you don't want to go to your place, let me take you to my apartment. The minute I know something, I'll call—"

"No."

"But—"

"I understand that because it's your sister, you feel the need to go yourself. Try to understand that Derrick's my cousin. If he's responsible for this, I need to be there, too. I need to do this for my family. For Emily."

"All right," Steven said. "But I don't want you tak-ing any chances. Now that I've found you again and we're so close to having a life together, I don't want anything to happen to you. Or to our baby. Promise me, you'll be careful and follow my lead.''

''I promise,'' Maria said and prayed that she'd be able to keep that promise as they exited the garage and headed out into the cold night.

Twenty-five minutes later they pulled onto the block and parked across the street from the apartment building. ''Why would Derrick rent an apartment here under an assumed name?'' she asked aloud.

Steven shrugged. ''Any number of reasons. He may have decided it was safer to meet here with Baronessa's competitors than to risk being seen with them in public or at their offices,'' he suggested. ''Or he may have been planning this kidnapping and ransom demand for a long time.''

''Derrick's never been big on planning or patience. Maybe Emily was right about him seeing a married woman.'' It certainly seemed to fit with her cousin's character. For as long as she could remember, he'd always wanted what someone else had.

Steven took out his cell phone, auto-dialed a number. ''It's Steven. I'm in Boston and I think I've found where Barone's holed up with Bianca.'' Steven held the phone away from his ear and Maria heard a man swearing on the other end of the line. ''You want to shut up a minute and let me give you the address or not?'' He rattled off the street and number, then replied, ''Too late. I'm already here and I'm going in.''

Maria heard the man yell, ''Conti! You son of a b—''

Steven ended the call and turned to her. ''Ethan and the feds are on their way. I need you to wait here, explain everything that's happened when they get here and tell them that Derrick may have a weapon.''

''But what about you?'' Maria asked. ''Where are you going?''

''Inside.''

''Steven, wait! Don't you dare go without me,'' she cried out, frustrated that her pregnancy caused her to move more slowly. She battled with the release catch on the seat belt. But by the time she'd disarmed the safety lock on the door and opened it, Steven was already across the street and running toward the apartment building.

Ten

Steven knew it was a lousy trick and that he'd probably have hell to pay later for tricking Maria as he had. But it would be a small price to pay to keep her safe, he reasoned. He'd meant what he'd said. He didn't trust Derrick Barone. It was bad enough the man had his sister. No way did Steven intend to let Derrick anywhere near Maria.

He waited for the couple he'd seen approaching the building to unlock the main door and enter. The moment they did, he dashed up the stairs and caught the door before it closed. Once the elevator doors closed behind the pair, he located the stairwell and then, taking the stairs two at a time, he started for the eighth floor. When he reached the fifth-floor landing, he checked his watch. Knowing Mallory, he figured he had maybe seven minutes tops before his former brother-in-law and the feds converged on the building. He just prayed that they'd manage to keep Maria away from Derrick's apartment.

Pulling open the door to the eighth floor, he started down the carpeted corridor. The place was as quiet as a church, he thought as he checked the numbers on the apartments on both sides of the hall in search of number 805. He found it at the end of the hall. From his quick glimpse of the building when they'd arrived and parked across the street, he estimated that the fire escape he'd seen was on the other side of the apartment. That meant the apartment door and the fire escape would be Barone's only exit routes, he reasoned. Adrenaline pumped through him as he pressed his ear against the door and listened for movement inside.

"Look out," Bianca screamed just as the door opened and Steven stumbled inside the apartment.

"Isn't it just like a sneaking Conti, listening at keyholes," Derrick told him with a sneer that emphasized his hawklike features.

But it wasn't the man's taunt that had Steven's heart in his throat. It was the sight of Derrick with his arm wrapped around Bianca's throat and a gun aimed at her head. "Let her go, Barone," Steven commanded.

"I'm the one calling the shots here, Conti. Not you," Derrick told him, waving the gun at him with jerky movements.

Still lying on the floor, Steven gauged his chances of rushing Derrick before he could get off a shot and decided it was a risk he couldn't take. Not with Barone still holding Bianca.

"Put your hands where I can see them and get up. Real slow."

Steven did as he said. He had never come face-to-face with a madman before, but he knew from the wildness in the other man's eyes that Derrick Barone was on the verge of snapping. "Why don't you put down that gun and let my sister go, then you and I can talk. Man to man."

Derrick laughed and the crazed pitch had the blood in Steven's veins running cold. "Unless you've got ten million dollars cash on you, we have nothing to talk about."

"I don't have it with me. But I can get it," Steven said, buying time. "But first you have to let my sister go."

"No," Derrick said and tightened his grip around Bianca's throat.

His sister coughed, clutched at Derrick's forearm to keep the pressure off of her windpipe. "You're choking me," she managed to get out.

"Let her go," Steven demanded and started toward him.

"Stay where you are," Barone shouted and aimed the gun at Steven. "I swear, you take another step and I'll shoot you and then her."

"Derrick, don't!"

Steven whipped around at the sound of Maria's voice as she came rushing through the door. "Maria, get out of here," he ordered.

"Well, well, well," Derrick said, a maniacal grin spreading across his face. "If it isn't my dear cousin. Back from your little vacation, Maria? And what's this," he continued, motioning to her belly with the gun. "Don't tell me that Baronessa's little sainted Maria has gotten herself pregnant? I wonder who the father is."

"Leave her alone," Steven said, stepping in front of Maria.

Derrick's gaze went from Maria to Steven and then

he laughed again. "Oh, if this isn't rich. I don't believe it. You went and got yourself knocked up by a Conti."

"Shut your mouth," Steven snapped. He curled his hands into fists at his sides, when what he wanted to do was smash them at Barone's face.

The laughing stopped. So did the smile. "No one tells me to shut up," he countered. "And no one gives me orders, not anymore. *I'm* the one who gives the orders now. Understand?"

"Understood," Steven said through gritted teeth. He needed to buy time, keep him talking until Mallory and the Feds arrived. "Why don't you put that gun down and we'll talk."

"I don't think so," Derrick told him.

Maria moved from behind him and faced her cousin. "Why, Derrick? Why are you doing this?"

Derrick laughed again. "Why do you think I'm doing it? For the money, of course."

"The ransom money?"

"God, but you're a stupid bitch," he said, disdain in his voice, in his expression. "How Grandmother could have picked you to run Baronessa is beyond me. Of course I did it for the ransom money. The way I figure it, you all owe me for the way you've treated me all these years. Ten million dollars will help me make a fresh start somewhere else, away from this stinking town, away from all of you."

Maria flinched at the venom in his voice. "My God, you really hate us."

"That's right."

"Is that why you set the fire at the plant?"

"Just covering my tracks, cousin. I couldn't let Carlo or anyone else find out that I'd been meeting with Snow-cream and offering to sell Baronessa's recipes."

"But you might have killed Emily," Maria accused.

"It's her own fault she got hurt. She wasn't supposed to be there. As it was, she screwed things up for me and I had to improvise."

"Improvise?" Steven said, noting movement out of the corner of his eye near the fire escape.

"Yes," Derrick said, a satisfied smile curving his lips. "I just blamed it on you Contis."

"How could you?" Maria demanded. "How could you have risked everything Marco and Angelica worked so hard to create? You could have destroyed our legacy."

"Not *our* legacy," he corrected. "*Your* legacy. And Daniel's and Emily's and Claudia's and all the rest of you."

"And yours," Maria insisted. "You're a Barone, too."

"No, I'm not. I'm Disappointing Derrick."

Steven caught sight of a second shadowy figure on the fire escape that he thought he recognized as Reese Jackson, one of the FBI agents on the kidnap case. He tried to pay heed to the conversation and prayed that Derrick wouldn't notice the activity.

"I'm the one none of you ever thought was smart enough to be trusted with anything important," Derrick continued.

"That's not true. You're a member of Baronessa's management team."

"A token job," he fired back. "*I* should have been the one at the helm of Baronessa. Not Nicholas or Joseph and certainly not *you*. I'm smarter than all of you. And I had good ideas, great ideas that would have put Baronessa on the map. But none of you would listen to me. Not Grandmother or Uncle Carlo or even my own parents. They all thought that Nicholas and Joseph and you were the smart ones who should run things. Well, you weren't. It should have been me.''

"Maria's listening now, aren't you, Maria?'' Steven said, not liking the way the man's arm tightened around Bianca's throat as he became more and more agitated. Nor did he like the way his tiny sister kept clutching at Barone's arm to keep the pressure off her windpipe. "Why don't you tell her some of those plans you have for the company now?''

"Yes,'' Maria said, obviously taking his cue. "Why don't you tell me about those plans now, Derrick?''

"It's too late,'' Derrick told her.

"No, it's not,'' Maria insisted. "Don't forget, I'm pregnant. My baby is due in February. I came back to tell the family and to resign.''

"They won't accept your resignation. You're their golden girl.''

Maria shook her head. "Not anymore. You know how much bad blood there is between us and the Contis. Once they know that Steven's the baby's father, I'm not sure they'll want anything to do with me.''

"Serves you right,'' Derrick told her.

"Regardless,'' she said. "Someone has to manage Baronessa Gelateria once I'm gone. That someone should be you.''

Derrick narrowed his eyes. "You're lying. You put Karen in charge when you went away. And when she left, you put her assistant Mimi in charge.''

"I made a mistake,'' Maria told him. "I'm sorry. I was wrong not to put you in charge of things. But we can fix that. I'll tell Nicholas and Uncle Carlo and everyone that you should have the job. They'll give it to you. I know they will.''

Derrick hesitated, his grip on Bianca's neck loosening. Steven eyed him closely, held his breath as the arm holding the gun lowered a fraction. He slid a glance to the window by the fire escape, waited for the Feds to make a move and swore silently when he saw the man with Jackson struggling to open the window. Damn them, he thought as an angry-looking Jackson said something to the other agent. They were going to blow it. Derrick might be crazy, but he wasn't stupid or deaf. He'd hear them. "Listen to her, Barone," he said, wanting to distract the man long enough so that he could charge him. "She's telling you that you can have what you want. You can be the top dog at Baronessa now. But that won't happen if you do something stupid and hurt Bianca or us. So why don't you put down the gun?"

"I'd be in charge of Baronessa?"

"That's right," Steven told him.

The window squeaked.

And Derrick went ballistic. He jerked his gun arm up, pointed it at Maria. "Liar! It was a trick. You tried to trick me."

"No, it wasn't," Maria insisted.

Glass shattered and Jackson and the other man came through the window shouting, "FBI!"

"Get back," Derrick yelled and Bianca screamed as he yanked his arm up and around her throat again. Tight. So tight, her face was turning red.

"FBI," Jackson said again as he rushed into the room. He aimed a gun at Derrick. "Put down the gun, Barone, and let the lady go. We've got the building surrounded. There's no way out."

"Wrong. I'm going to walk out of here and she's going to be my ticket," Derrick said, yanking Bianca tightly against him and causing her to gasp for breath. "Call them off now or I swear I'll snap her neck."

Bianca started to choke again. She clawed at Derrick's arm and Steven saw blood, but the man seemed oblivious to his injuries. "For God's sake, do it," Steven shouted at Jackson, fearing for his sister's life.

"Pete, tell the team to stand down," Jackson called out.

"Now you put down your weapon," Derrick ordered as he waved his gun at the agent. When Jackson hesitated, he tightened his arm around Bianca's throat.

"All right," Jackson said, putting his weapon down on the floor in front of him.

"Him, too," Derrick said, motioning to the other agent. Once he'd complied, Derrick told them, "Real slow now. I want you to slide them over here toward me. And I swear if you try anything, I'll snap her neck and put a bullet in my cousin."

"All right," Jackson said after he and his partner had done as instructed. "Now why don't you let the lady go?"

"I don't think so," Derrick said, a feral look in his eyes. "I told you, she's my ticket out of here. Now I want you to—"

Suddenly Bianca elbowed Derrick in the gut and when he grunted, she followed through with a karate back kick to his shin that sent him stumbling back against the wall. Maria screamed. Bianca swung free, spun around and karate kicked his arm. Steven and Jackson both rushed toward Derrick, but Barone was already on his feet, waving the gun wildly at them.

"Get back," he screamed. "Get back or I'll start shooting. I swear I'll do it." Steven and the agents froze. "Now all of you, move over there together."

"Give it up, Barone," Jackson said as he and his partner moved near him and the two women. "There's no way out for you now."

Derrick's gaze darted from one to the other. His eyes were those of a madman, Steven thought. The arm that Bianca had kicked drooped and was covered with bloody scratches. He began backing up, moving toward the broken window to the fire escape.

"Listen to the man, Derrick," Maria pleaded. "Put down the gun before anyone else gets hurt."

"No," Derrick said. "I'm not going to jail."

"Derrick, please," Maria tried again as her cousin reached the window and began to climb out onto the fire escape.

"Don't do it, Barone," Jackson said.

Suddenly Steven realized what Derrick intended. "You're making a mistake," Steven told him, not wanting Maria and his sister to witness what was about to happen. "You don't have to do this."

"Yes, I do," Derrick told him. He put his other leg through the window. "I told you, I'm not going to jail," he repeated. "I can't."

And then before anyone could stop him, Derrick jumped off of the fire escape and sent his body plummeting into the dark, cold street below.

Later as she stood on the sidewalk bundled up in Federal Agent Reese Jackson's coat and watched the medical examiner load Derrick Barone's body inside the coroner's wagon, Bianca felt as though she were awakening from a nightmare.

"That was a very brave and very stupid thing you did up there," Agent Jackson told her, censure in his deep voice and in his green eyes. "You could have gotten yourself killed."

"But I didn't," Bianca informed him, miffed to have him chide her for defending herself.

"No, you didn't," he said with a scowl. "But you could have. What in the hell were you thinking, pulling those karate moves on a man twice your size? You're lucky he didn't snap that pretty neck of yours in two."

"Luck had nothing to do with it," she fired back. "I knew what I was doing. I have a black belt in karate."

"I don't care if you've got ten black belts, what you did was stupid. You shouldn't have risked it."

Bianca bristled. "It was my neck," she informed him. She didn't care if the man did look like Brad Pitt, she didn't need some macho agent admonishing her. "And instead of criticizing me, you might want to thank me for saving your neck."

"My neck?"

"That's right. If I hadn't done what I did, Derrick might very well have shot you and your partner."

"What's going on here?" Steven asked as he walked up to the two of them with Maria by his side.

"Agent Jackson and I were just discussing whether or not he should be thanking me for saving him from taking a bullet in that handsome face of his."

"Oh God," Maria said and turned her face into Steven's shoulder.

"I'm sorry," Bianca said, regretting her sharp tongue. Now that her ordeal was over and her fear had subsided, so had her initial shock upon discovering that Maria was the woman her brother had been seeing.

"It's all right," Maria told her. She took the handkerchief that Steven offered and swiped at her brown eyes still bright with tears. "I'm the one who's sorry for what my cousin did."

Compassion stirred in Bianca for the young woman pregnant with her brother's child. "I hated Derrick for what he put me and my family through. But I didn't expect..." She swallowed. "I didn't want to see him dead."

Maria nodded. She looked up at Steven. "I'll need to tell Emily and Aunt Sandra and Uncle Paul what's happened to Derrick."

"You should go with her," Bianca told him.

"But we need to let Mom and Dad and Aunt Lucia know that you're okay," Steven said.

"I'll do it."

"All right. Tell them I'll call them later. I think it's time we arranged for a meeting between both families," Steven told her. "And the sooner, the better."

"That's probably a good idea," Bianca replied. But she didn't envy her brother or Maria the task ahead. Aside from everything that had happened, she didn't imagine news of Steven and Maria's relationship would make either family happy. She looked at the couple, saw the depth of love between them. Reaching out, she touched her brother's arm. "Whatever happens, I'll support you. Both of you."

"Thanks. I appreciate that."

"Me, too," Maria added.

Steven smiled. "Come on, I'll bring you home and then Maria and I need to go see Derrick's family."

"You two go on. I'll see that your sister gets home safely," Agent Jackson said.

"That's not necessary," Bianca scoffed. "If you'll just call me a taxi—"

"I said I'd take you," Jackson insisted. "After all, it's the least I can do, seeing as how you saved my handsome face."

Maria exited the ladies' room of Antonio's the next morning at the sound of Lucia Conti's voice. Nerves began in her stomach as she peered around the corner at the scene.

"Answer me, Steven. What is the meaning of this?" Lucia demanded. "Why have you insisted we come here this morning? And what are the Barones doing here?"

"I'll explain everything in a moment, Aunt Lucia."

"I'm sorry we're late," a sad-eyed Emily said as she entered the restaurant with Shane Cummings.

Maria's heart swelled with sympathy at the sight of her cousin who moved to stand beside her grief-stricken parents, Daniel and his wife, Phoebe, and Derrick's sister Claudia. Despite everything that had happened, they had all loved Derrick.

"Everyone's here now," Bianca said as she joined her brother. "And I've told the staff that the restaurant won't be open for lunch today."

"You did what?" a red-faced Salvatore Conti asked. "Have you forgotten that this restaurant is our business?"

"No one's forgotten, Father. But this is more important," Steven told him.

"Listen to him, Daddy," Bianca added.

"All right. I'm listening," Sal told them.

"By now most of you know about last night's tragedy," Steven began, and as Carlo and Moira wept, he, Bianca and Emily related the chain of events leading up to Derrick's suicide.

"I loved my brother," Emily told them. "And while it breaks my heart to admit that he was capable of doing such deceitful, hurtful things, it was Derrick who sabotaged Baronessa's. It was Derrick who set fire to the plant, kidnapped Bianca and pretended to be kidnapped himself. Derrick was guilty, but he knew we would blame the Contis,'' she continued, tears streaming down her cheeks. "And we did blame them."

When Emily's mother began weeping aloud, Maria pressed a fist to her breast to ease the ache she felt for her aunt.

"Emily, can't you see you're upsetting your mother? What's the point of rehashing all this now?" Uncle Paul demanded.

"The point is that Derrick was sick and while nothing can excuse what he's done, maybe if he hadn't been able to feed on our distrust of the Contis, things would never have gone so far. And maybe," she said, her voice breaking, "maybe he wouldn't be dead now."

"You are blaming us for Derrick's death?" Maria's father asked incredulously.

"I'm blaming all of us, Uncle Carlo. You, me, all of us," she told him, sweeping her arms in a broad gesture. "We should never have allowed this stupid feud between our families to go on all these years."

"The Barones are not the ones who started the feud," Carlo informed her.

"Your father and mother started it when they betrayed me and my brother," Lucia countered, her dark eyes flashing brightly in contrast to her pale face and white hair.

"It doesn't matter who started it," Emily countered. "The point is we've all kept it alive." She turned to the Barones. "We suspected the Contis of being saboteurs, of kidnapping and arson. It's time for it to stop. I want the feud to end now."

"And how do you propose we do that, child?" her uncle asked.

"By taking the first step. By apologizing to the Contis for blaming all of our misfortunes on them."

When stunned silence followed, Maria feared it was a lost cause and then her oldest brother, Nicholas, said, "My cousin is right. It's time for this feud between our families to end." Then he marched over to Sal, Jean and Lucia Conti. "You have my apologies," he said to them. When no response was forthcoming, he repeated the phrase to Bianca and Steven, who nodded their assent.

"My son and niece are right. It is time for this feud to end," Carlo said and Maria wanted to run out and kiss her father when he stepped forward to stand before the Contis. "I believe I speak for all of us here and for my daughter Maria as well when I say that we were wrong to suspect your family and to blame you for our misfortunes. Please accept our apologies."

Sal Conti made no attempt to take Carlo Barone's extended hand. Lucia pursed her lips into a disapproving scowl, then folding her arms, she turned away. There was no mistaking the insult or the angry flush burning her father's cheeks. Maria's heart sank. If their families couldn't even get past an apology, what chance was there that they would accept her and Steven together?

"I accept your apology, Mr. Barone," Steven said, breaking the tense silence. He took her father's hand, shook it.

"So do I," Bianca said, echoing her brother.

"What do you think you're doing?" Lucia hissed at the pair.

Steven faced his aunt. "There's been enough bitterness between our families. It's time to end it."

"No," Lucia cried out.

"Steven's right," Bianca added. "Let the bitterness end now. Accept the Barones' apologies."

Sal Conti looked at his wife. She nodded and taking her husband's hand she walked with him over to the Barones, where they shook hands first with Carlo and Moira Barone, then with Nicholas.

Steven turned to his aunt. "It's time to bury the past, Aunt Lucia. Accept the olive branch the Barones have extended to us, put an end to all these years of hatred. The Conti/Barone feud is over and we have all suffered enough because of it. Declare the curse null and void and let us be done with it."

"I will do no such thing. Have you forgotten what the Barones have done to me? To our family? They kidnapped your sister and accused us of sabotage when all the while it was one of their own."

"The man responsible is dead. So are Marco and Angelica Barone. What good will come of keeping this anger and hatred for them alive? It's time to forgive them and move on."

"Never," Lucia told him. "I will never forgive them for what they did to me. Do you have any idea what it was like to have the man you loved, that you planned to spend the rest of your life with, run away with the woman you thought of as a sister?"

Although Maria knew Lucia Conti to be eighty-four, the pain in her voice, in her eyes, belonged to a young girl. And Maria couldn't help but feel sorry for her. Any hopes she'd harbored that Lucia might accept her and remove the threat of the Conti curse withered.

"Aunt Lucia," Sal Conti interceded. "Steven is right. A young man is dead. It might well have been our Bianca. It is time for us to put an end to the hatred. Do as Steven asks. Accept the Barones' apology and call off the curse.''

Lucia waved her nephew's remarks aside. ''I'm sorry the boy's dead. But a few pretty words and tears cannot make up for the wrongs we Contis have suffered at the hands of the Barones all these years.''

''Aunt Lucia,'' Bianca began.

''Enough,'' Lucia said, making a slicing motion with her hand. ''You do what you want. But I see no reason why I must accept their apology or nullify the curse.''

''Then I'll give you one,'' Steven told her. ''Maria,'' he called out.

Nervous, Maria stepped from around the corner wall where she'd been hiding and walked over to join Steven on legs that felt like jelly. She heard the gasps of surprise, could feel all eyes on her swollen belly. But she kept her gaze fastened on Steven who held out his hand for her. When she reached him, he held her hand tightly in his, kept her close by his side.

''You want a reason to end the feud and void the curse, Aunt Lucia. Here is your reason. I love Maria, and the child she's carrying is mine.''

Maria barely heard the shocked gasps or the whispers that sounded around them. Her total attention was on the old woman clad in funeral black who gripped the cane she held so tightly, Maria feared the bones in her fingers would snap.

''You have betrayed me,'' she said, her voice and expression filled with venom.

''I have not betrayed you. I love you,'' Steven told her. ''That's why it's important to me that I have your blessing and that you agree to end the curse.''

Lucia shook her head. ''Never. Never!''

''You said you needed a reason. I've given you one.

The baby Maria carries is half Barone. But it's also half Conti. We, Maria and I, want you to be the baby's godmother. Are you willing to let your godchild come into this world with a curse on his or her head?''

Lucia's lips trembled. Her dark eyes searched out Maria. "Is what my nephew says true? Do you want me to be your child's godmother?''

Maria stepped forward, took Lucia's thin, wrinkled hand into her own. "It's true. And if the baby is a girl, we plan to name her Lucia Angelica after you and my grandmother.''

"What do you say, Aunt Lucia? Will you be our baby's godmother?''

Tears misted Lucia's eyes for a moment. Still holding Maria's hand, she released her cane and captured Steven's hand. "Yes. And I, Lucia Conti who called down a curse upon the Barones and their descendants, hereby declare the curse forever void.''

Cheers went up and suddenly her parents and Steven's parents, her sisters, brothers, cousins and extended family were all flocking around them and asking a dozen questions at once.

"When is the baby due?'' her mother asked.

"I didn't even know you knew Steven Conti,'' her sister Rita chimed in.

"Now I understand why you weren't feeling well at the family reunion,'' her sister-in-law Gail told her.

Suddenly the rapping of Lucia's cane brought all conversation to a halt.

"What's wrong, Aunt Lucia?'' Steven asked.

"I want to know why everyone is wasting time, asking a bunch of silly questions when we have a wedding to plan.''

"Your Aunt Lucia's right," Steven's mother, Jean Conti, said. "You are going to get married, aren't you?"

"Absolutely," Steven said and hugged Maria close. He asked her the same question with his eyes.

"Absolutely," she replied, her heart filled with love and hope.

"Then we need to get busy," Lucia said, taking charge. "The first thing we need to do is have Moira Barone use that Reardon family clout of hers and get the Church to waive the bans so that these two young people can be married right away. Because I refuse to have my godchild born out of wedlock. And you'll have to forgive me, Maria, but from the looks of things," she continued, pointing at her rounded belly, "that baby could be arriving at any time."

"Moira will make a call to the Monsignor right away," Carlo offered.

"Forget the monsignor," Moira replied. "I'll call the archbishop."

Her mother called the archbishop. And the following weekend just before Christmas she and Steven became man and wife in the chapel before God and assorted members of the Conti and Barone families. The end to the seventy-year-old feud and curse had been the only wedding gift she and Steven had wanted. But her mother and sisters had insisted on a small reception after the ceremony. The size of her family alone made a small reception nearly impossible, Maria mused as she surveyed the more than thirty guests gathered in the hotel banquet room. For a moment, she felt a pang of sadness as she thought of her cousin Derrick. His death and betrayal had devastated them all. And she certainly would

have understood if her aunt and uncle and cousins had
opted not to attend the wedding or the reception.

"My secretary told me that every caterer and musician
in the city was already booked through the New Year,"
Steven said, dragging her thoughts away from the past.
"How on earth did your mother manage to pull this off
on such short notice and with Christmas next week?"

"You don't know my mother and cousin Claudia.
They can charm just about anyone into doing anything."
And they apparently had, Maria thought as she swept
her gaze over the elegantly decorated room. Tables had
been draped in ivory damask. Chairs had been covered
in matching damask and tied at the back with elegant
bows. Red and white roses with baby's breath spilled
from crystal vases. Poinsettias, in red and white, seemed
to be tucked in every corner of the room. A six-tiered
wedding cake trimmed with sugar roses sat atop a table
with real rose petals scattered at the base. An ice sculpture bearing the Baronessa logo sat next to a gelato sta-
tion, where she'd been told by Karen that the passionfruit flavor was being renamed True Love in honor of
her and Steven's wedding. It pleased her to see that another ice sculpture bearing the Conti logo had also been
created for the reception.

"Maybe I can convince them to come work for me,"
Steven teased.

"Not much chance of that," Maria informed him.
"My mother's far too busy with my father and Claudia's
already on every charitable committee you can think of.
Besides from what my sisters tell me, your friend Ethan
has plans for Claudia's future."

"So he does. Did you know they're planning a Valentine's Day wedding?" He smiled and touched her
belly. "That's going to be a busy day."

"Are you okay with their engagement?" she asked. "I mean since he was married to your sister?"

"I'm fine with it. He and Bianca weren't right for each other, but Ethan's still a great guy."

"And Bianca?"

"It doesn't seem to be a problem for her."

Maria looked over to where her new sister-in-law stood with federal agent Reese Jackson. "I think you're right."

"But I'm far more interested in you than in my sister," Steven told her. "Have I told you what a beautiful bride you are?"

"Yes," Maria said, laughing. "Several times in fact. Although I don't know how you can think that when I look like I'm carrying a basketball."

"Easily. Because it's true. You are beautiful, Maria," he said, his face suddenly serious, those blue eyes of his moving over her like a caress. "And I love you with all my heart."

"And I love you," she replied, moved by the sincerity in his voice.

When the band began to play, he leaned close and whispered, "Dance with me, Mrs. Conti?"

"Of course," she told him and as Steven led her to the dance floor, she thought of that very first dance they had shared at Nicholas and Gail's wedding nearly a year ago. But then he took her into his arms and Maria forgot all about their families. As he waltzed her around the room, she forgot all about the feud that had caused so much pain. She forgot about the Conti curse and her fears. She forgot about everything except for Steven and the happy life that stretched out before them. And she knew in her heart that she and Steven and both their families had been granted their own special Christmas miracle.

Epilogue

Maria handed baby Lucia over to Bianca, whom they had asked to serve as a co-godmother to their child when Aunt Lucia had insisted she was too old to accept the honor and responsibility at her age. But judging from Steven's aunt's attitude since the baby's birth seven weeks earlier, Maria suspected Lucia Conti might well outlive them all.

Assured her baby was in good hands, Maria slipped out of the patio doors and into the garden away from the buzz of the christening party going on inside. Feeling happy and at peace, she breathed in the spring air and the scent of April blossoms. The roses, daisies and tulips had shaken off winter's chill and now basked in the early April sunshine.

Sometimes she still found it hard to believe that her life had been so blessed these past few months. And chief among those blessings had been Steven and the birth of their daughter, Lucia Angelica Conti.

"Where's my goddaughter?" Nicholas called out, and Maria turned her attention back to the party going on inside the house where the din of happy voices seemed to grow louder by the minute.

She spied Steven talking to Reese Jackson, the federal agent who had become a constant presence in Bianca's life since the night she had been rescued. Call it female intuition, but judging from the hungry way the handsome agent watched her sister-in-law, Bianca's days as a single woman were numbered.

Scanning the room, she easily picked out her sister Rita from among the guests, recognizing her older sibling because of her height, as well as the tall, handsome accessory she sported—her husband, Dr. Matthew Grayson. She watched the pair laugh at something Flint, her sister Gina's husband, said. When Alex, decked out in his Navy uniform, joined the other couples with his wife, Daisy, and their own little Angel in tow, Maria couldn't help thinking of how things had worked out for the two of them. It also made her think of her grandmother Angelica. She could almost hear her grandmother telling her, "When God closes one door, He opens a window."

Her grandmother had certainly been right, she mused as she noted her sister Colleen and Gavin O'Sullivan. Who would have thought that after her sister had left the convent that she would reunite with her college sweetheart? Or that when Nicholas hired Gail as a nanny for little Molly that they would fall in love with each other and marry?

Maria continued to scan the guests and noticed the most recent newlyweds—her cousin Claudia and Ethan Mallory—sharing a quiet moment off by themselves.

Then Maria smiled at the sight of her brother Reese and his wife, Celia, talking with her parents. After years of estrangement, it was wonderful having Reese back in the family fold. It was also wonderful to see her brother Joseph happy again—which she fully attributed to Holly, the pastry chef who had finally helped her brother get past the loss of his wife.

When she saw Emily, Maria was relieved to note that her eyes no longer held that haunted look as they often had since Derrick's death. No doubt her marriage to fireman Shane Cummings had helped her move beyond her grief, Maria surmised. Even Daniel, Derrick's twin who had been so somber and eaten with guilt following his brother's death, seemed happier than she'd seen him in months. And from the way he was looking at Phoebe, she knew that his wife was responsible.

When a very pregnant Karen excused herself from Ash and the Calderones and headed in her direction, Maria was filled with affection for the long-lost cousin who had been her confidante and closest friend during most of her pregnancy. "Decided to abandon the party?" she asked as Karen joined her outside.

"Hardly. I thought I'd let Ash regale the Calderones with all the information he's been beefing up on regarding pregnancy and childbirth and find out why you're hiding out here."

"Not hiding, just reflecting," Maria responded.

"No more worries about the curse, I hope."

"None," Maria assured her. The birth of her daughter on Valentine's Day had forever wiped away any fears she'd had on that score. Lùcia Angelica was healthy, happy and perfect in every way. Her birth had also cemented the budding relationship between her and Steven's families.

"That's a relief. I was worried you wouldn't be able to let go of all those old superstitions about Valentine's Day being unlucky for the Barones."

"Oh, I'm still superstitious," Maria informed her cousin and grinned when the other woman arched her brow. "Now I'm convinced that Valentine's Day is a lucky day for us Barones."

"I'll buy that," Karen said with a chuckle.

At the roar of laughter from indoors, both Maria and Karen shifted their attention to the group where a grinning Steven was getting an earful from Aunt Lucia.

"Wonder what that was all about," Maria said.

"Looks like we'll know soon enough," Karen replied as Steven approached.

"Hello, Karen," he said when he reached them.

"Hello, Steven. Congratulations. Little Lucia is beautiful."

"Takes after her mother," he replied in that dark, velvety voice that always made Maria's pulse jump.

"I, um, I think I'll go see if I can find Ash," Karen said and excused herself.

"What was that all about?" Maria asked. "It looked like your Aunt Lucia was reading you the riot act."

"She just wanted to let me know that she thought it was time we started working on a baby brother or sister for little Lucia." Steven smiled at her and slid his arms around her waist to draw her close. "I promised her that I'd get right on it."

Maria groaned and dropped her head against her husband's chest.

"Have I told you lately how much I love you?" he asked.

"Yes." And she never tired of hearing it. "I love you, too."

"I don't know about you, but I'm eager to get started on making that new baby. So what do you say we go cut that christening cake, reclaim our daughter and head for home?"

"Sounds like a plan to me." And as they joined their families and basked in their love and joy, Maria thought once again of her grandmother, could almost feel her presence.

If I have but one wish for you, my Maria, it's that someday you will find true love as I did," her grandmother told her. *"That you will know what it is to live passionately with the man you love."*

I've found it, Grandmother, Maria whispered in silent answer. I've found my true love. And she knew as she twined her fingers with her husband's that with Steven, she would live passionately ever after, just as her grandmother had wished.

*   *   *   *   *

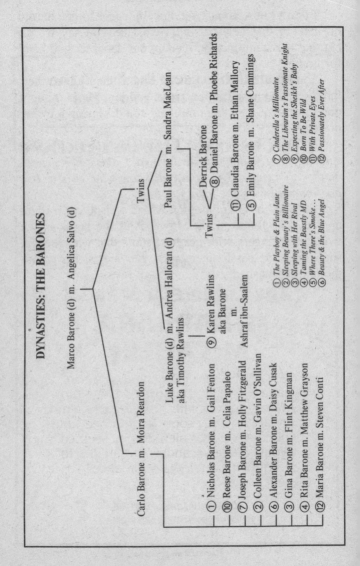

DYNASTIES: THE BARONES

Marco Barone (d) m. Angelica Salvo (d)

Carlo Barone m. Moira Reardon

Luke Barone (d) m. Andrea Halloran (d)
aka Timothy Rawlins

Twins

Paul Barone m. Sandra MacLean

① Nicholas Barone m. Gail Fenton
⑩ Reese Barone m. Celia Papaleo
⑦ Joseph Barone m. Holly Fitzgerald
② Colleen Barone m. Gavin O'Sullivan
⑥ Alexander Barone m. Daisy Cusak
③ Gina Barone m. Flint Kingman
④ Rita Barone m. Matthew Grayson
⑫ Maria Barone m. Steven Conti

⑨ Karen Rawlins
aka Barone
m.
Ashraf ibn-Saalem

Twins

Derrick Barone
⑧ Daniel Barone m. Phoebe Richards

⑪ Claudia Barone m. Ethan Mallory

⑤ Emily Barone m. Shane Cummings

① The Playboy & Plain Jane
② Sleeping Beauty's Billionaire
③ Sleeping with Her Rival
④ Taming the Beastly MD
⑤ Where There's Smoke…
⑥ Beauty & the Blue Angel

⑦ Cinderella's Millionaire
⑧ The Librarian's Passionate Knight
⑨ Expecting the Sheikh's Baby
⑩ Born To Be Wild
⑪ With Private Eyes
⑫ Passionately Ever After

Silhouette®

Desire.

is proud to present the first in the
provocative new miniseries

DYNASTIES : THE DANFORTHS

A family of prominence…
tested by scandal,
sustained by passion!

with

The Cinderella Scandal
by BARBARA McCAULEY

Tina Alexander's life changed when
handsome Reid Danforth walked into
her family bakery with heated gazes aimed
only at her! They soon fell into bed…but
neither lover was all that they seemed.
Would hidden scandals put an end to
their fiery fairy-tale romance?

Available January 2004
at your favorite retail outlet.

The Stolen Baby

Silhouette Desire's powerful miniseries features six wealthy Texas bachelors—all members of the state's most prestigious club—who set out to unravel the mystery surrounding one tiny baby...and discover true love in the process!

This newest installment
continues with,

Remembering
One Wild Night
by KATHIE DeNOSKY

(Silhouette Desire #1559)

Meet Travis Whelan—a jet-setting attorney...
and a *father?* When Natalie Perez showed up
in his life again with the baby daughter he'd
never known about, Travis knew he had
a duty to both of them. But could he
find a way to make them a family?

Available January 2004 at your favorite retail outlet.

eHARLEQUIN.com

For **FREE online reading,** visit
www.eHarlequin.com now and enjoy:

Online Reads
Read **Daily** and **Weekly** chapters from
our Internet-exclusive stories by your
favorite authors.

Red-Hot Reads
Turn up the heat with one of our more
sensual online stories!

Interactive Novels
Cast your vote to help decide how these
stories unfold…then stay tuned!

Quick Reads
For shorter romantic reads, try our
collection of Poems, Toasts, & More!

Online Read Library
Miss one of our online reads?
Come here to catch up!

Reading Groups
Discuss, share and rave with other
community members!

For great reading online,
visit www.eHarlequin.com today!

COMING NEXT MONTH

#1555 THE CINDERELLA SCANDAL—Barbara McCauley
Dynasties: The Danforths
Tina Alexander had always lived in the shadows of her gorgeous sisters, so imagine her surprise when Reid Danforth walked into her family bakery with heated gazes aimed only at her! Soon the two fell into bed—and into an unexpected relationship. But would this Cinderella's hidden scandal put an end to their fairy-tale romance?

#1556 FULL THROTTLE—Merline Lovelace
To Protect and Defend
Paired together for a top secret test mission, scientist Kate Hargrave and U.S. Air Force Captain Dave Scott clashed from the moment they met, setting off sparks with every conflict. Would it be only a matter of time before Kate gave in to Dave's advances...and discovered a physical attraction neither would know how to walk away from?

#1557 MIDNIGHT SEDUCTION—Justine Davis
Redstone, Incorporated
An inheritance and a cryptic note led Emma Purcell to the Pacific Northwest—and to sexy Harlen McClaren. As Emma and Harlen unraveled the mystery left behind by her late cousin, pent-up passions came to life, taking over their senses...and embedding them in the deepest mystery of all: love!

#1558 LET IT RIDE—Katherine Garbera
King of Hearts
Vacationing in Vegas was exactly what Kylie Smith needed. The lights! The casinos! The quickie marriages? Billionaire casino owner Deacon Prescott spotted Kylie on the security monitor and knew the picture of domesticity would be perfect as his wife: Prim in public, passionate in private. But was Deacon prepared to get more than he bargained for?

#1559 REMEMBERING ONE WILD NIGHT—Kathie DeNosky
Texas Cattleman's Club: The Stolen Baby
Waking from amnesia, single mother Natalie Perez knew her child was in danger. High-powered lawyer Travis Whelan was the only man who could protect her daughter—the man who had lied to her and broken her heart...and the father of her baby. Would the wild attraction they shared overcome past betrayals and unite them as a family?

#1560 AT YOUR SERVICE—Amy Jo Cousins
Runaway heiress Grace Haley donned an apron and posed as a waitress while trying to get out from under her powerful—and manipulative—family's thumb. Grace just wanted a chance to figure out her life. Instead she found herself sparring with her boss, sexy pub owner Christopher Tyler, and soon her hands were full of more than just dishes....

SDCNM1203